The Forgiven Scoundrel

The Forgiven Scoundrel

Laura A. Barnes

Laura A. Barnes
2020

Copyright © 2020 by Laura A. Barnes

All rights reserved. This book or any portion thereof may not be reproduced or used in any manner whatsoever without the express written permission of the publisher except for the use of brief quotations in a book review or scholarly journal.

First Printing: 2020

ISBN: 9798669192921

Laura A. Barnes

Website: **www.lauraabarnes.com**

Cover Art by Cheeky Covers

Editor: Polgarus Studios

To Krystal Komro,

Thank you for taking the time to brainstorm with me during NaNoWriMo on ideas for Belle's story. You're the BEST!!!

Prologue

Rosalyn stared out the window, jumping at every movement. Her gaze searched the lane for any sign of Phillip's arrival. He was late. Phillip had promised they would meet this afternoon. She had much to tell him. Rosalyn hoped the joy of her news would bring him the same happiness as she felt. She rested one hand on her flat stomach and smiled. The hour grew late and her need to return home grew closer. But not before Rosalyn spoke with her true love.

    The last few months spent in Lord Phillip Delamont's company had been the most enjoyable time in her life. Rosalyn had never expected to hold a love for another so deeply. The word love didn't even come close to the emotion she held for Phillip. He was the other half of her soul. She'd known this from the moment their eyes met, the touch of his hand when they danced, the first taste of his kiss invading her senses. The world spun with Phillip in Rosalyn's universe. She reflected on Phillip's care when they made love for the first time. His gentle, loving nature. His passion. Phillip held himself back for her pleasure until Rosalyn's curiosity convinced him she wasn't a fragile miss. Rosalyn's smile widened, recalling the pleasure Phillip showed releasing his passion. Phillip left no part of her untouched. His kisses, his touch, and the whisper of his voice, wrapped Rosalyn in love.

A flicker outside the window caught Rosalyn's eye. She peered out from behind the drapes, admiring Phillip riding his horse to the front of the cottage. Rosalyn's anticipation intensified at the sight of him. His muscular thighs gripped the horse, while his sandy locks blew in the air. Phillip had let his hair grow longer through these summer months. Rosalyn couldn't wait to brush the hair behind his ears while she welcomed Phillip with a kiss. She whirled away from the window, rushing through the open door to fly into his arms. Phillip caught her and held Rosalyn close. His grasp tightened before abruptly pulling away.

Rosalyn, too caught up in his appearance, didn't notice Phillip's serious demeanor. She laughed at his attention and smoothed her dress, trying to press out the wrinkles. Since Phillip had arrived later than they'd planned, Rosalyn would need to leave soon, before her parents discovered that she had snuck away. She would share the news with Phillip and then agree to meet him later after her parents retired for the evening. Rosalyn grabbed his hand and tried to pull him into the cottage. When Phillip wouldn't budge, she turned.

"Phillip?"

Phillip stared at Rosalyn. There were no words to describe what he must do. He must give her no reason to doubt him. Every cell in his body wanted to gather her close and never let her go. Phillip wanted to spend the rest of his life showering Rosalyn with love. To kiss her lips every morning and devour her body long into the night. She was the very air he breathed. However, his wishes would be forever denied, because of circumstances out of his control. Phillip would never get to awaken with Rosalyn by his side again. Never watch her grow with a child. Never hold her hand.

Phillip took in every inch of Rosalyn. From the moment they met, he had fallen under her spell. Her smile had fooled him. He'd never expected the desirable, sassy, lovable chit packaged under the sweet innocence. From every witty remark to every whisper of love, Rosalyn stole his heart. From every strand of her fiery hair, to her flashing green eyes, to her long lovely legs he wanted to worship at her feet. She would always be Belle to him. It was the special name given to her by him after they first made love. She rang the bell to his heart. Phillip noticed Rosalyn held a secret that she wanted to share with him, but he refused to hear it. It would only make his declaration that much harder to say. What he was about to do would crush her soul. Phillip knew what *his* news would do, because at this moment his soul was torn apart with bitter resentment.

Rosalyn's excitement disappeared at the seriousness in Phillip's gaze. When he wouldn't respond, Rosalyn stood on tiptoes and tried to press a kiss to his lips. Any other time, this would have loosened her serious lord's manner. Only this time was different. Phillip didn't return the kiss, instead pushing her away to stalk across the room. The rejection cut deep. It was as if her touch revolted him. Rosalyn wrapped her arms in front of her. Phillip turned and raked her from head to toe, glaring at her appearance. This was the same judgmental stare Phillip's father had done to Rosalyn the week before, when Phillip made the introductions at his family's annual ball. Now, Rosalyn took a step back in shock. When his glare continued, she dropped her arms. Rosalyn returned Phillip's stare, refusing to be intimidated by his aristocratic air. His father might have made her feel unworthy, but she wouldn't allow Phillip to treat her with the same disregard. There must be an explanation for Phillip's behavior. After Phillip had begged for forgiveness, Rosalyn would announce the news.

When Rosalyn stood proudly before him, Phillip knew in his heart she would survive. *He* might not, but Rosalyn would. Rosalyn's resilient character would endure the heartache about to unfold. How Phillip craved to take those pinched lips under his until they melted. To wrap his arms around Rosalyn and reassure her of their love. To have the hostility evaporate. To strip away the dress tightened around her curves and make love one last time. Phillip moved forward before he realized it. Her eyes lit with forgiveness, and this became the fuel to destroy their relationship. Rosalyn forgave too easily. She needed to stand strong with her anger towards his behavior.

When he advanced, Rosalyn thought Phillip had let go of whatever infuriated him, but she was mistaken. Rosalyn could never have prepared herself for the onslaught of pain Phillip would deliver.

"Our time together has come to an end. My father will have the banns read this Sunday for my marriage to Lady Julia Minturn. Since we are to wed within a month's time, I need to settle my affairs. I cannot be caught amusing myself with the lower gentry. It would not be fair to my intended. I realized what a mistake you were when I invited you to my family's annual ball. Your inadequate manners and the status of your family made me aware of how unsuited we could ever be. While you have made my time in the country this summer a delightful affair, that is all it ever was. You, my dear, have been a fetching piece of baggage, and I have thoroughly enjoyed teaching you the finer points of lovemaking. Your innocence whetted my appetite to many pleasures that I will find hard to deny myself. But deny I must."

Rosalyn paled at his cruelty, swaying back and forth. She might even have whispered the word *no* over and over, but nothing passed from her lips. Instead, the denial was shouted inside her head. Rosalyn's heart broke into a million pieces when Phillip's words continued to drone on. His nonchalant attitude confirmed a belief in everything he said. He meant every single word. The coldness in Phillip's gaze froze Rosalyn still.

Phillip realized he'd convinced Rosalyn when the light vanished from her eyes, replaced by a blankness never seen before. Phillip had to leave now, before he crumbled and admitted to the lies, unable to keep the truth from Rosalyn. With one final look to last him a lifetime, Phillip strode past Rosalyn. When she choked out a sob, Phillip paused at the door. Rosalyn's pain echoed around him.

"Phillip," she whispered.

He closed his eyes. Phillip flung the door open and continued to his horse, not once looking back. He climbed onto the saddle and urged the horse into a sprint. He needed to put distance between them.

No matter how far away Phillip traveled from the cottage, the broken pieces of Rosalyn's heart followed, clinging to his soul.

Rosalyn followed Phillip to the door where she watched him fly away down the country lane. Her legs gave away, and she sank to the floor. Rosalyn leaned her head against the door jamb. Tears trailed along her cheeks, landing on her clasped hands which gently rubbed her stomach, trying to help ease the pain. But the ache would never disappear. The man who she gave her heart to, who she loved with every fiber of her being, had dismissed her as one would a servant.

Phillip had never loved Rosalyn as she loved him. Rosalyn had thought she knew the true Phillip. Wasn't he the other half of her soul? The words he'd spoken couldn't be real. A nightmare rocked Rosalyn's world. One she would wake from soon while Phillip held her in his arms, soothing her with loving words. Belle brought one hand up and touched her heart.

Yes, all would be well. Rosalyn had yet to tell Phillip the exciting news. Once she awoke she must tell him. They were to have a baby. A baby created from their love for one another.

Chapter One

Mid-afternoons were Belle's favorite part of the day. They were a time where she could slip away unnoticed by the staff and everybody else in London. These moments she regained sanity from her hectic life. Belle unwound from the previous night's activities and prepared for the evening to come.

Ned, her man in charge, wanted Belle to take an escort on these walks, but she refused. When she ventured out, she was no longer Madame Bellerose, the notorious brothel and gaming hell owner. No, she was Rosie, a widow enjoying the fresh air. She walked the line in two separate worlds. While she held friendships with many of the peer, she was a pariah to others. This wasn't how Belle imagined her life would be when she was a young innocent girl, but it was the life she now lived, making a living supporting herself and many others. Her girls and guards were family. They were more of a family to Belle than one she was born in to. Her parents had thrown her out because Belle made the mistake of giving her heart and body to a man whose primary intent was a bit of fun. Belle no longer held resentment for the past or those who'd wronged her. She overcame the sense of abandonment with the help of a dear friend. If it weren't for Alexander Langley, the Duke of Sheffield, the path of Belle's life would have destroyed her in the end.

Belle didn't really understand why she wanted to reflect today. She thought to have put the past behind, but with the recent wedding of her dear friends she had turned sentimental. All her past sufferings and imagining of what could have been consumed Belle. The only thing she wouldn't let herself remember was *him*. Belle wouldn't even speak his name. The pain would be too intense. It still consumed her at times. Especially those moments when she wanted to be held in a man's tender embrace. Many gentleman had made offers through the years, and tempting as they were, Belle had refused them all. Why she still saved herself for *him*, Belle held no clue.

Belle walked over to a favorite bench in the park and sat down. The ton didn't frequent this area; only the working class of London. The shopkeepers, professionals, and the lower gentry. As the regular visitors passed, they would stop and speak a few words before they carried on. None of them knew her actual identity. Belle wore a simple day dress that hid her curves, sensible shoes, and her hair laid in a long braid hanging down her back. She refused to wear a bonnet.

"Hello, Rosie."

"Hello, Poppet."

Belle smiled at the little girl holding her mother's hand. The mother struggled to try to hold onto a babe in her arms. Belle pulled Ashley on her lap while the tired mother sighed with relief before she sat down. Belle's heart ached for Claire. Her husband worked the dock and they could barely afford to feed their children, let alone own a baby basket to carry the child. Belle had made an offer to help, but Claire refused. When pride was all one had, it was best to let them keep it. If not, it could lead to their downfall. Belle understood that only so well.

Ashley chatted gaily about the new ball Papa bought for her birthday. Ashley pointed across the park at her brother sharing the ball with a new friend. Belle watched Nicholas playing with a boy she had never seen before. She turned to Claire to inquire about the lad, but Claire mouthed *later*. Belle nodded and opened a paper sack. She peeked inside, then looked at Ashley. The little girl giggled, enjoying the game they always played.

"How lucky we are that I brought three biscuits with me today. Perhaps your brother's new friend would like one too?"

"Let me go ask, Rosie. I will be right back."

Ashley crawled off Belle's lap and ran across the open lawn toward the boys. Belle chuckled at her excitement.

"You should not spoil them so."

"Pssh. A biscuit does not spoil a child. Do not take my enjoyment away, Claire."

"I'm sorry. The babe is teething and kept me awake all night."

Belle smiled in sympathy. She ran a hand over Joshua's soft hair. The old familiar ache tugged at her heart. An ache never to be relieved. The pain had resurfaced with friends starting their families. Recently, Dallis and Rory had welcomed a baby girl named Morgan, and now Kathleen and Devon were expecting a child in a few months. It was only a matter of time before Sidney and Sophia would become pregnant too. Not an ounce of envy Belle felt, only happiness for them. However, the ache of never holding her own child made Belle melancholy.

"So, spill the story before they come for their treat."

"I am not sure who the boy's father is. But he made the mistake of hiring Alice Timmons," said Claire.

"She is the worst governess in London."

"Yes, there is no doubt about that. From what I can gather, he is an influential peer of the ton. The poor boy lost his mother earlier this year and his father has returned to London to take his seat in Parliament. Alice said his late wife detested the town life, so they resided at their country estate. With his wife dead, he came to resume his old life."

"Where is Alice? And why did she bring him to this park?"

"She is fooling around with the stable hand in the park mews, hence the reason they are here."

"The poor lad. I wonder who his father could be?" Was Belle acquainted with the gentleman? Alice was always one to brag if she gained a position with a prestigious family.

"That remains a mystery. Alice is keeping silent on who her employer is. She calls the boy Henry. She told Mrs. Hoppington that the lord will pay her a generous bonus if she keeps quiet on his status."

"Why such secrecy?"

"Rumor is the boy is not his, but a bastard. The lord only married the woman to give the child his name. They *were* engaged to wed, and she fooled around with another. The lady cuckolded him before becoming his bride. The poor man. However, he has raised the son as his own, which makes him honorable in my eyes."

Belle hadn't heard of any gentleman returning to London from the country. Her heart went out to the boy already painted by scandal at such a young age. A stigma he would wear his entire life. Even his father suffered from rumors and innuendos. If the gentleman wanted to remarry, he would meet resistance by many. They wouldn't want their daughters attached to any scandal. Most gentlemen in his position would want to marry again to gain a spare. Belle would make inquiries with Sheffield into which lord had returned to town. Why she felt a curiosity was a mystery. Perhaps it was because the child held a sadness about him, missing his mother.

Before Belle responded to Claire, the children had clamored to her side. She smiled at them when she opened the sack, offering them each a biscuit. Ashley and Nicholas thanked her under their mother's guidance. But Henry hung back, not attempting to take the remaining treat. Belle held the bag out.

"No, thank you, ma'am. It would be highly improper of me to take your last biscuit."

His manners and offer of courtesy impressed Belle. For one so young, to think of another implied the discipline in which he was being raised. Belle smiled, holding the bag out farther. She could tell Henry wished to eat the treat by the longing glances he gave Ashley and Nicholas.

"But I bought it for you."

"How so? You have never met me before."

"Yes, but I always buy biscuits for Ashley, Nicholas, and their friends. I might not have known of you, but I knew they would have a friend near."

"Go ahead, Henry. Rosie is swell, she always spoils the children in the park," said Nicholas.

Still the boy wouldn't stick his hand in the bag.

"Would you reconsider if we split the treat? For I cannot eat the entire thing by myself. Would you be agreeable to that, Henry?"

"Yes, ma'am. I suppose that would be fair."

Belle broke the biscuit in half, offering the bigger piece. Soon the kids were running off eating their treat at the same time.

Henry stopped and ran back. "Thank you, Rosie," he said hesitantly, unsure if he should call her by name or not.

"You are most welcome, Henry."

His face lit up and Belle lost what remained of her heart. She fell in love with the sweet boy. Henry reminded Belle of herself. Lost.

Belle watched the children play while she caught up with Claire. Soon they watched Alice gather her charge and leave. After Claire and the children left, Belle remained for a few more minutes. She closed her eyes, letting the peace of the park soothe her soul before she returned home. Belle would need to hurry and change before any customers arrived. This time in the park today lasted longer than usual. Maybe she should retire to the country? The hustle and bustle of the city was starting to take its toll. While she'd enjoyed it for years, now Belle only wanted open skies and fresh air. Or maybe just time away. Belle had thrived in the city. The excitement of London made her come alive. But she would ask Sheffield if the offer of his home along the coast was still available.

Belle walked back along the path, the sun starting its descent into the night. She headed back to the life that differed so much from the one she portrayed as Rosie.

~~~~

"You are late, boss."

"I know, Ned. Please fill me in."

Ned explained who was on duty and which guests had arrived already. With the season not in full swing, most families were still away at their country estates. That left the gentleman bored and seeking attention. Belle gave further directions to Ned then started back to the office.

"Sheffield awaits you in your private parlor," Ned called after her.

"Why did you not tell me earlier?"

"Because he said he would wait until you were available, when I told him you had not returned from your walk."

Belle nodded and then hurried to the parlor. She missed her friend. The need to be in the company of somebody who understood her grew stronger.

"Alex, my dear, I was not aware that you had returned to town."

Sheffield rested on Belle's sofa, nursing her fine whiskey. She had the stiff drink smuggled in to cater to the clientele. Sheffield's long limbs stretched out on the sofa, like he used to when he was a customer and bored with London's delights. Since his marriage to Lady Sophia Turlington, Sheffield never graced the brothel again. Once in a blue moon, he would play cards. But not often. Belle missed his companionship. Why did she still remain so sentimental?

"Yes, Sophia wanted to welcome Dallis and Rory's newest addition. Do not tell Sophia, but I suspect she is jealous of Sidney getting the baby all to herself."

"Your opinion is safe with me."

Belle sat across from Sheffield. For years she would rest beside him and lay her head on his shoulder while they shared their problems. Other times, he would just hold her, always knowing when she needed affection. It felt strange not to do so now.

Sheffield frowned at Belle's pensive mood. Any other time she would tease him unmercifully. However, this evening he sensed Belle's melancholy when she entered the parlor. Now she sat across from him, lost. The hell with propriety, Sophia would understand. Rather, she would scold him for not offering affection sooner. No prying eyes would witness it. Nobody dared to enter Belle's private chamber without permission.

Sheffield patted the space next to him.

"No, those days are behind us, Sheffield."

"No, they are not and will never be. The dynamics of our friendship has not changed, nor will it."

"What about Sophia?"

"I can hear her now, berating me for not offering sooner. She would have her arms open if she were present. Now come over here. I can tell you are in need of a hug."

"I'm sorry, but I must refuse your offer of comfort. It would not be proper."

Sheffield's laughter shook his shoulders. "There has never been one moment of our friendship which has ever been proper. So why should we change the course of it now?"

"Because you are a happily married man. You are no longer a bachelor who can disregard the standards of society."

"Belle, I am a duke. I can do whatever the hell I want. And right now I want to offer comfort to a friend in need. Either you move your beautiful body or I will come to you."

Belle rolled her eyes at his arrogant tone. Sheffield had to have every situation his way. Reluctantly, she sat down beside him. He pulled Belle to his side like always, holding her close. Sheffield stroked a hand up and down her arm, soothing away the sense of loss consuming her all day.

"What is it, love? What has caused you to look like you lost your best friend? Since I am here, I know that is not the case."

"I miss him something fierce today. I have tried not to think of him and I refuse to say his name. But for some unknown reason I cannot stop myself from reminiscing of our time together."

"Ah, Belle." Sheffield was at a loss on how to respond. From time to time Belle would reflect on the past. He was glad he stopped by for a visit. When these moods overcame Belle, she would become depressed for days on end.

Belle snuggled deeper into Alex, seeking the comfort he gifted her with. She would confess to Sophia and beg forgiveness later. Now she only wanted to savor the affection of someone who cared. Sheffield whispered inconsequential comments to distract her, soothing tattered emotions.

"There was a lad at the park today, playing with the Parker children."

Sheffield knew of Belle's walks through the park nearby. Belle shared with him about the outings and the people she befriended over the years. People that meant nothing to him, but he listened patiently anyway. He understood the time Belle spent away from the brothel was healthy for her wellbeing. Sheffield remained quiet, waiting for Belle to continue. This boy must have been the catalyst for her unstable emotions.

"I would judge his age to be around seven years old. He was very polite and held a look of profound sadness. I learned he had recently lost his mother." Belle explained about the biscuit incident and how she watched the lad play. "The boy would have been around the same age as …" Belle choked back a sob, but couldn't contain the tears.

Belle was racked with sadness, remembering the time in her life when she most wanted to disappear. Sheffield pulled her on his lap, wrapping both arms around Belle, trying to soothe her anguish. There were no words that could prevent this sadness. All the memories came flashing back in a tidal wave of images. The happiness of discovering her pregnancy. The secret rendezvous to tell her lover the news, and instead being informed of his betrothal to another. The heartbreak endured at the betrayal. How her family disowned Belle. Sheffield's kind offer of friendship and support. Every single memory of the child growing in her body, and a love that grew stronger than anything she experienced before. Then the horror of a difficult labor, every recollection of loss and death. Her precious baby. Not only had Belle lost the love of her life, but the only connection left of him too. If it weren't for Sheffield, Belle didn't know where she would be today. Belle owed him more than ever could be repaid.

"His name is Henry. Is it strange that I felt a connection to him, something that cannot be explained?"

"No, my dear, it is understandable. You have much in common."

"I hope to see him again."

"Do you think that would be wise? Perhaps you should visit another park, my dear."

"Henry needs showing that somebody cares. Obviously, the boy's welfare does not concern his father, considering the poor choice of the governess hired to look after him."

"Belle, you would be opening yourself to a heartache that would not be good for your state of mind."

Belle wrapped a hand around his cheek and smiled sadly. "But if it would ease his heartache, I can endure the pain. He is but a child."

Sheffield kissed her palm. "You have a heart of gold, Belle. Now tell me more of this boy you wish to befriend."

There would be no persuading her otherwise. Sheffield decided he must keep a close eye on Belle during this friendship with the boy. He needed to discover the identity of the child's father and convince him to hire a better governess. Sheffield had watched Belle throughout the devastation of losing her child and the man who Sheffield once considered a friend. Sheffield would do whatever he had to do to protect Belle.

Belle talked to Sheffield late into the night. It was the first time that she had ever neglected her business. Her newfound energy directed toward helping a little boy was the only thing she thought about. When the hour grew even later and Sheffield should have returned home, he continued to keep Belle company. Even when she drifted into a slumber.

Sheffield watched the beauty fall asleep in his arms. Her loveliness like no other. Well, except for his wife, Sophia. The man who Belle had gifted her heart didn't deserve such devotion. He had destroyed Belle at her most vulnerable and he didn't even remain to pick up the pieces. Sheffield had, and he would continue to do so. While Belle was an attractive woman, he'd never crossed that line with her. Their strong relationship, never physical, was held together emotionally. He would protect her to the end. Sheffield rose and carried Belle into the bedroom through a secret door. He laid her on the bed and pulled up the covers. Sheffield knew she wouldn't rest for long, but hoped she would. The dark circles under her eyes were proof of many sleepless nights. Sheffield would enlist Sophia's help to encourage Belle to use their home along the coast. Belle needed to get away before she became too attached to a certain young lad.

Chapter Two

Belle smiled, walking inside her home after time spent at the park again. She'd found Henry alone and looking scared from being left unattended. No other children played because of the light drizzle. The poor boy sat drenched and was near tears. Belle sat next to him and soon had him giggling. An umbrella shielded them from the light rain. They shared all the biscuits, since the Parker children wouldn't be at the park. Her heart already felt lighter. When Alice finally returned to gather the boy, Belle pulled her aside and scolded her on neglecting her charge. But Alice looked down her nose at Belle and told her to mind her own business. Well, Belle would not. She'd forgotten to ask Sheffield to find out who the boy's father was; she would send a note now.

Belle entered the parlor, intending to write the request, and she pulled up short. Four beautiful women and one baby had invaded the room. A delightful baby who cooed at her entrance. Belle's face lit with joy that her friends had come to visit. However, the shocked look on their faces was confusing her. Every lady sat with their mouth wide open, and looked back and forth between them, hoping somebody could explain. Explain what?

"Hello, ladies. What do I owe this unexpected pleasure?"

Sophia rose and wrapped Belle in a hug. "I missed you while I was away. When I called on Dallis yesterday to see her precious bundle, she informed me you had not called to see the new babe. So we decided to come to you. We understand why you will not visit us, even though we disagree."

Belle returned Sophia's hug. "I have missed you also, all of you. I have wanted to visit the babe, but I do not want to bring scandal to your families."

"Pssh. What nonsense," Dallis replied, settling the babe in Belle's arms.

Belle gazed at the child who seemed to smile at her. The creature was precious. In awe, she moved to sit on the sofa, cradling the child close. Her finger rubbed along the softness of the baby's cheek. A tear slid down Belle's face unnoticed.

"Belle?" Dallis asked.

Belle raised her eyes to their concerned gazes. A wistful smile did nothing to dismiss their concern. "She is adorable."

Sophia had sent a secret message to everyone. Alex had urged her to invite the women to Belle's, but wouldn't tell her why. He mentioned how he'd paid Belle a visit and that she needed her friends. When Sophia asked Alex to explain why, he refused, telling her it wasn't his story to tell. Sophia contacted everybody, and they'd rushed over, hoping the babe would help with whatever troubled Belle. But it did the opposite, causing Belle to cry. Belle wasn't herself, that was more than obvious. Even down to the style of her dress, which shocked them when Belle strolled into the parlor.

This wasn't the ravishing beauty who had captivated them when they first met her. They had never seen Belle in anything other than a form-fitting dress hugging her curves, hair falling graciously around her shoulders with a curl dangling near her breasts. Instead, before them now was a lady dressed in a simple blue day dress with hair pulled back in a braid. Belle appeared years younger. When Sophia looked closer, she understood that this was who Belle truly was, not the professional act Belle needed to portray for business. This was a gently bred lady who led a simple life.

Dallis gathered and passed the baby to Kathleen. Dallis's relationship with Belle differed from Sophia and Sidney's. However, from their first meeting a connection that could never be explained strengthened their friendship. Dallis believed something from Belle's past haunted the beauty. She gathered Belle's hands after she'd dried away the tears.

"Belle, we come as your devoted friends out of concern. Please allow us to help you through your troubles, as you have helped us with ours."

"You are too kind, Dallis. All of you are, to come to me in my time of need. Sheffield sent you, am I correct?" She directed her question to Sophia.

"Yes, he said you needed us, but did not tell me why," answered Sophia.

"I assumed as much. But as excited as I am to visit with you, you need not trouble yourself on my account. I suffered a slight setback, but all is well."

"Bull," Sidney said.

"Excuse me?" Belle arched an eyebrow.

"You heard me correctly, my lady."

Belle's sarcastic laughter filled the room. "My lady?"

"Yes," they all replied.

Belle paused, humbled by their adamant answer. She looked at each lady and the determination on their faces. They meant to discover her secrets and Belle wouldn't be rid of them until they knew. She should have known Sheffield would sabotage her with these ladies. Nay, friends.

"Belle?" Sidney urged.

"Very well. Where shall I begin?"

"The beginning is usually the best place," Dallis said, squeezing Belle's hand for encouragement.

Belle feared she would lose each lady's friendship after they heard her story. She couldn't bear any more loss. Before she told her sad tale, Belle decided to test the water with Sophia first.

"Before I begin, I want to offer you my apologies for the previous evening. During Sheffield's visit he offered me comfort that I sought, in my selfishness, to have a man hold me in his embrace. I took advantage of your friendship by seeking such comfort from your husband's arms."

"Please stop stalling, Belle, and confide in us your sorrow. If my husband gave you the comfort you needed, then I am proud that he cared for a friend. I know nothing untoward happened between you two. I trust both of you with my heart. So you will not scare me away. Now spill."

"We all feel that way, Belle," Kathleen said.

Belle looked each one of them deep in their eyes and saw how they considered her. She was their friend. Because of these ladies' husbands, Belle now held a friendship with them too.

Belle opened her heart, telling them how her life came to be. Every joy, every heartache. Every high, every low. They each took a turn holding her hand and drying her tears. She finished the story with the newfound joy of meeting Henry at the park, and how she had taken him under her wing. However, she'd carefully never revealed Phillip's identity, and they knew better than to ask.

"Oh, Belle, we never imagined," Sidney said.

"How can we help?" asked Sophia.

"Can you have Sheffield inquire to whom the boy's father might be? I would like to meet and explain to the gentleman how he has hired an incompetent governess."

"I will have Alex try to discover his identity. Do you think it will be wise to confront this gentleman? He could hold enough power to destroy you."

"But I hold a lot of power in my own right, Sophia. Plus, I have many influential friends."

"Perhaps, after we find out who this gentleman is, I can host a dinner party that you must come to," Sidney said.

"One of your dinners would not be the best thing for Belle," Dallis said.

"Nonsense, it is time to be rid of her feelings for this mystery scoundrel of her past and meet a new gentleman to make her happy. She has already fallen in love with his son. Who is probably a small replica of his father. It would be perfect," Sidney argued her case.

"Sidney, I know your heart is in the right place, but I do not think Belle wishes to entangle herself with your matchmaking," Sophia said, expecting that Belle would never entrust her heart to anyone again.

"Who was he, Belle?" Kathleen asked, despite herself. "The man who hurt you?"

"I made a promise to myself to never speak his name again. It hurts too badly."

"All the more reason to move on. While we all offer our husbands for you to use for comfort, you need a man to *love* you. If you know what I mean." Sidney waggled her eyebrows.

All the women gave into a fit of laughter. Sidney always lightened the mood with her quirky sense of humor. Belle held out her arms again to hold the babe. As the ladies enjoyed their tea and cake, Belle relaxed and enjoyed the simplicity of the moment. Today she only wanted to savor the gift of friendship. Tomorrow was another day.

Chapter Three

Phillip sat in the dark, watching his son sleep. He'd never thought he would love the boy like he did, but Henry was his life. The heartache they both shared bonded them closer than ever. His beloved Julia had been gone for a few months, but they still grieved as if she only passed away yesterday. The sadness lurking in Henry's eyes grew every day. Phillip had hoped that by coming to London, a change of scenery would alter their emotions. It only made Henry miss home more. Home, what a farce. It had been a prison to Phillip since the day he wed Julia. Because of another man's mistake, the chains bound him to a life he didn't wish for. Recently, Phillip kept recalling a past that was but a distant memory. Sometimes he wondered if it had only been a dream. Something he had imagined to help him survive.

Phillip called Julia his beloved because in time she *had* become that to him. It wasn't her fault, the circumstances which led to their wedding. They settled into a comfortable marriage of friendship. For that, she was his beloved. A beloved friend that had met an early demise. Julia didn't deserve the suffering she had endured. Phillip missed her, now more than ever.

Over the last few days, Henry's demeanor had changed. A positive change that Phillip hoped would continue. Henry had made a friend at the park. A girl named Rosie. How ironic that Henry would befriend somebody with a name similar to the only woman Phillip ever loved with his soul. Did he think of the past, because of the familiarity of the names? It took him back to a time when he had never been happier.

Phillip still remembered Rosalyn; the way she gifted him with a smile every time he teased her. She'd enjoyed his attentions, and he enjoyed returning them. Even now, Phillip remembered every second of their time together.

However, he needed to forget that past. He didn't deserve to enjoy those memories because of the heartache he'd caused Rosalyn.

Phillip rose with one last glance at Henry before he retired to his study. He would check with Alice on who Rosie's parents were. Perhaps invite them over for luncheon one afternoon. It wouldn't hurt for him to make connections with the parents of his son's friends. If it made the transition easier for Henry, then that was what Phillip must do.

He settled in a chair near the fire, nursing a glass of brandy. Who was he trying to fool? Himself? There wasn't a day in the last eight years that he didn't think of Rosalyn. At first he ached for a chance to see her and explain, but he couldn't. Then after the wedding, he settled into a daily life with thoughts of Rosalyn kept at bay. However, after Julia died, those thoughts consumed every waking moment again. Hell, really, Rosalyn was the reason he uprooted their life. Phillip used the excuse of taking his seat in Parliament, and that's all it was. An excuse. He came to London for her. He'd learned from village gossip, Rosalyn had moved to the city. His old friend, Sheffield, had stepped in, taking his place quickly enough. Phillip knew Sheffield held a special place in his heart for Rosalyn—or more like his pants. Sheffield's lustful urges for Rosalyn never went unnoticed. Phillip didn't fault her over falling for Sheffield's charms. Phillip later discovered that Rosalyn's family disowned their daughter because of her involvement with him. In truth, Phillip couldn't even hold anger at Sheffield. If Sheffield provided for Rosalyn's welfare, then he owed his friend a debt of gratitude.

He planned on paying a visit to Sheffield on the morrow. There he hoped to learn Rosalyn's whereabouts. Phillip heard Sheffield had married Lord Turlington's daughter. So, knowing his friend as he did, Sheffield would have retired any mistresses. Sheffield was an honorable man who wouldn't betray a wife. Phillip's guilt dug deeper in his gut, knowing that he'd led Rosalyn down the path of sin. He'd taken her innocence and left Rosalyn all alone. Phillip never meant to, and wanted them to be together forever. However, fate played a cruel game. Fate was an evil mistress. It would tempt you with all that your heart desired and then snatch it away.

Julia had known of his love for Rosalyn and always urged Phillip to tell the truth. But it was not his truth to tell. A truth that Phillip would keep hidden. For it would destroy the livelihood of Henry. No, Phillip himself would die before ever uttering that truth.

~~~~

The butler held the door open for Sophia as she arrived home. She handed her gloves and bonnet to Mason, inquiring as to her husband's whereabouts.

"He is in his study with Lord Beckwith and Lord Wildeburg."

Before Sophia could inform Mason to send the gentlemen into the library when their business was concluded, a knock sounded on the door. She nodded for Mason to answer it, showing that she would wait. Mason held the door open to a tall, distinguished gentleman who held the hand of a small boy.

"Lord Phillip Delamont, here to see Alexander Langley." The gentleman announced, handing his card to the butler.

The butler took the card and showed them into the foyer. Sophia stepped forward.

"I will see to Lord Delamont and his companion. Please inform His Grace to join us in the library."

"Very well, Your Grace," Mason said.

"If you will, please follow me," Sophia said, heading toward the library.

Once Sophia settled, Lord Delamont bowed and urged Henry to do the same. "I did not mean to intrude, Your Grace."

"You are not intruding. Please take a seat while we wait for Alex. Now, how are you acquainted with my husband?"

"We are old friends."

"I am afraid my husband has never mentioned you. You must tell me all about your friendship, Lord Delamont."

"Please allow me to introduce my son. His name is Henry. I am sorry, I am at a loss, I do not know your name."

Her musical laugh pulled a smile from his son. "It is I who am sorry. I ushered you away from Mason and rattled on without introducing myself. My name is Sophia, all my friends call me Phee."

"It is our pleasure to make your acquaintance."

"Do tell me about yourself. I have not seen you around London."

"We have only recently arrived in town."

"Well then, I must host a dinner to welcome you. Maybe I can call on your wife tomorrow?"

"I am afraid my wife is no longer with us. She passed away a few months ago."

"I am sorry for your loss. Please forgive my pushiness."

"There is nothing to forgive, Your Grace. You did not know. I do not think Sheffield even knows. As I mentioned before, we were friends long ago, and have not kept in touch. I had hoped to renew our friendship again."

"Do you plan to stay long or will you be returning to your estate?"

"My plans are undecided until I resolve a conflict from my past."

Sophia's curiosity grew. Who was this gentleman? Sophia's glance kept straying to the young boy. He held the manners of a proper young gentleman, not moving an inch, except for his eyes. They kept straying toward the books. She sensed he wanted to explore the titles. His eyes held a look of sadness, which reached and tugged at Sophia's heart. She wanted to wrap her arms around him and hug him dearly. The poor mite had suffered a tremendous loss at such a young age.

"Do you like to read?" Sophia asked Henry.

Henry looked to his father for permission to talk. At his father's nod, the boy's smile shone.

"Yes, my lady."

"Your Grace," his father corrected.

"Sorry, Your Grace."

"Your Grace is too formal of a term for me. Please call me Phee."

Henry looked to his father again. Phillip nodded his permission. This lady went against every trait he would have expected for Sheffield to require in his wife. The lady was the epitome of grace, from the tone of her speech, to her manners and style of clothing. She was not pretentious. Phillip assumed that Sheffield's wife would be a haughty shrew, to match the personality of her husband. Instead, the Duchess of Sheffield was a sweet-natured woman who made them feel welcome. Sheffield's wife was exquisite.

"Yes, Phee. I love to read," Henry answered.

Sophia stood and held out her hand. "Come."

Henry settled his hand in Sophia's and she led him toward the back corner of the library where Sheffield kept books for young children. They had been adding to their collection in recent months after their friends started having children, hoping they would be parents soon too. Meanwhile, Sophia wanted their home to be inviting for their friend's children.

"Perhaps, you might find a title here you would like to read, while your father talks with my husband."

Henry ran the tips of his finger over the spines. Sophia listened to him whispering the titles. When he found one he liked, he pulled it from the shelf. Sophia pointed to a chair where he could read. Henry crawled into the sprawling leather chair, opening the book and running his fingers over the words he absorbed. Sophia smiled, the picture of his innocence bringing her joy.

She rang the bell before she rejoined Lord Delamont.

"Your son is a delight. You must be proud."

Lord Delamont looked at Henry. Pride didn't even describe what he felt for the lad. The emotions of pride, love, and heartache all rolled into one.

"Very much so."

"So, you were about to tell me about your friendship with Alex."

Before Phillip answered Sophia, Sheffield strolled through the door. He was flanked by two other gentlemen. One Phillip recognized to be Wildeburg, the other gentleman he didn't know. The man didn't look like one Sheffield would befriend, but then Sheffield surrounded himself with a different crowd from when they ran together in their youth.

Sheffield paused, regarding him with a look that Phillip couldn't quite decipher. It was a cross between slugging him for all his mishaps or slapping him on the back to welcome his return. He hoped the latter, for he didn't want to cause a scene in front of his son or the duchess.

"Delamont, you old devil. You have returned to London." Wildeburg saved Phillip from Sheffield. Wilde was always the one to step in to prevent a scuffle. Wilde glanced between both men, sending them each a silent message to behave. Delamont shook Wilde's hand.

"Yes, I have come to claim my seat in Parliament and to show my son, Henry, the city."

Phillip gestured that his son was in the room, so that nothing inappropriate would be said. He would admit that he'd brought Henry here for that very reason, and that he felt a coward because of it. Sheffield glanced at the boy in the corner reading a book and nodded.

"Since you are acquainted with Wilde, please allow me to introduce Lord Roderick Beckwith." Sophia noticed the tension filling the room from the minute her husband stalked inside.

After Sophia made the introductions, Rory took his leave. Wilde stayed near, hoping to keep things civil. But neither man would waver. Finally, after another of Sheffield's curt replies, Wilde made his excuses and left, shooting Sophia an apology. She smiled and told him she would call on Sidney later, for they had much to discuss. Sheffield and Wilde both knew that was code for gossip and trouble. Sheffield saw the wheels turning in his wife's mind. It wouldn't take long for her to put two and two together. He already had when Delamont mentioned the boy. This was the young lad Belle had met in the park. And Delamont was the father who had ripped out Belle's heart. The heart that he'd try to help heal. When Sophia returned from Belle's yesterday, she had more information on Belle's young companion. Belle requested for Sheffield to inquire on who the father may be. Sheffield agreed, hoping that if he introduced the two, Belle would find happiness with the lord. Oh, he understood how the ton would frown upon a brothel owner moving into their circles, but then Belle deserved every bit of happiness that their small group of friends had found. If it weren't for Belle, they would never had found their soul mates. But now that Sheffield knew who the father was, he would sell his soul to the devil so that Belle would never meet Henry's father.

All the anger Sheffield held for his past friend came rushing forward. The only thing that kept him from pounding the man was his wife and Delamont's son. Sheffield wanted Delamont to pay for every minute that Belle had suffered—and still suffered to this day. Once Beckwith and Wilde left, he wanted to drag Delamont to his study, but got interrupted by the tea cart wheeling in. Sophia smiled at Sheffield, sensing his anger and wanting to calm him. She came to his side, sliding her hand through his arm. Sheffield sighed and settled Sophia on the sofa, sitting down next to her. He held out his hand, indicating for Delamont to take a seat. Sophia poured them tea and called for Henry to join them. Sophia introduced the boy to Sheffield, and he spoke a few kind words to the lad.

Sheffield looked the boy over and noticed the similarities from Lady Julia and a few of Delamont's attributes too. He'd learned that Delamont had sired a son, a fact Sheffield never shared with Belle. If Belle were ever to discover that while she lost her child, this boy had lived, it would destroy her. Sheffield thought he knew Delamont. But even Sheffield had been clueless to Delamont sharing his bed between two women. What had fooled Sheffield even more was that he believed Delamont loved Belle with the same undeniable love that Sheffield held for Sophia.

However, Sheffield would never misjudge this man again.

"Look, Papa. These are the same biscuits I shared with Rosie at the park yesterday. Except she had cherries in hers."

"Who is Rosie?" Sophia asked.

"A young friend that Henry has befriended at the park. She is all he speaks about." Delamont smiled at his son.

Sheffield saw the moment that the connection clicked in Sophia's head. She glanced at him, and he shook his head to stay quiet seeing that she wished to utter her realization out loud. Then, as soon as she realized the full impact of the situation, he saw those same gears clicking at a rapid speed. Sheffield needed to put a stop to this before all hell broke loose.

"Why have you called, Delamont?" Sheffield snapped.

"Alex," Sophia reprimanded him.

"It is all right, Your Grace. I understand Sheffield's anger and he is correct in displaying it. I had hoped we could discuss the whereabouts of—"

"That topic is none of your concern," Sheffield said, before Delamont uttered Rosalyn's name.

"I understand that you hold the opinion that the matter is none of my business. I would still like a private word with you to discuss it. No offense, Your Grace," Delamont said to Sophia.

"None taken. Please, Alex, take Lord Delamont to your study. I will keep young Henry company while you have your discussion. We have many biscuits left to devour." Sophia winked at the boy.

Sheffield placed a kiss on Sophia's cheek. "Do not get any ideas," he whispered fiercely in her ear.

"None?" she innocently asked.

"None," he growled.

Sophia only smiled her sweetest smile. The same smile that always brought Sheffield to his knees. Once Sophia smiled, he never denied her wishes. Ah, hell.

Sheffield strode from the room, expecting Delamont to follow him. He slammed the door behind them, pacing back and forth in front of the fireplace.

"What in the hell are you doing in London?"

"I think you already know the answer to that question."

"Absolutely not."

"Why? Is she still your mistress? Your wife is a stunning beauty, I would not expect you to stray from her."

Sheffield advanced on Delamont, pulling him by the cravat and sticking his face in his.

"You will not disrespect my wife in that manner again. Nor will you disgrace Rosalyn. I can tell you are still as arrogant as ever."

"It takes a gentleman with the same traits to recognize those in another. Hell, I learned every bit of them from you. You were the master of arrogance and I see you still are. Except now, there is a softness in your manner. Who has caused that, Sophia or Rosalyn?"

This time Sheffield didn't hold back, swinging his fist and planting it right in Delamont's eye. Then he dropped his hold of him as if the lord soiled him. Now Sheffield understood Beckwith's satisfaction when he'd slugged him. The need to seek vengeance for a friend felt empowering.

Phillip said, "I deserved that and probably more. My apologies for slandering your wife's good name. I let the past get the better of me, and my jealousy fueled my need for spite."

Sheffield said nothing, still waiting for Delamont's explanation as to why he came to London. He wouldn't say any more. Sheffield wouldn't give Delamont the information he sought.

"Julia has passed away, and I have come for Rosalyn. I've heard that she resides in London and you have knowledge of her whereabouts."

"Rosalyn has no need of your company, nor would I allow you anywhere near her."

"Does your wife know how protective you are of your ex-mistress?"

Sheffield growled, not rising to Delamont's bait. If Delamont thought Belle had been his mistress, Sheffield saw no need to speak the truth of their relationship. He wouldn't lie—at one time he desired to make Belle his. But at her refusal, he never tried again, instead nurturing the friendship that he held with no other. Except for Sophia.

"Sophia is well aware of my relationship with Rosalyn and even considers her a friend of her own."

Delamont paused at this. What kind of lady was Sophia to allow a relationship between Sheffield and Rosalyn to continue? He took Sophia for a generous woman, but not that generous. The duchess must still be an innocent and she allowed Sheffield to bully her into believing that nothing untoward happens between him and Rosalyn.

Even now, Delamont wasn't angry with Rosalyn for seeking comfort from another man. He'd led her to this life. However, the anger that stirred in him toward Sheffield only made him want to hurt the man. Any way that he could.

"How could you?"

Sheffield sighed and sat behind his desk.

"How could I what?"

"How could you take what was mine and make it yours? You had no right."

"Did I not?"

"How long did it take after I left for you to conquer Rosalyn between your bed sheets?"

"Delamont, you lost all rights to Rosalyn when you pledged your vows to another woman."

"My father demanded that I take Lady Julia for a bride."

"At one time I considered you my greatest friend, but now Rosalyn holds my devotion of friendship. I pledged to protect her. Even from you."

"I would never hurt her."

"You can honestly stand there and think your past actions did not hurt her deeply? You wounded her so much that no other man has enjoyed the woman she's become."

"Her pain must not have run too deeply for her to spread her thighs for *you*."

That was all it took for Sheffield to explode from his chair and advance on Delamont. This time he didn't hold back with one punch. Sheffield's fists exploded one after another on Delamont. This time, Delamont didn't stand there and let Sheffield beat him. He threw his own punches, both of them trying to cause the other pain.

~~~~~

"Henry, how do you like the chocolate ones?"

"They are yummy." He spoke with his mouth full.

Sophia laughed.

"You have a pretty laugh like Rosie."

"Your friend from the park?"

"Yes. You are pretty like her too. And you both give me biscuits."

"Tell me more about Rosie."

"She makes me feel special, like mama used to. I enjoy talking with her."

"Where is your governess during this time?"

"Alice is off with her friend in the stables. She told me to stay put and not wander away."

Henry told Sophia how the pretty Rosie talked to him, telling him stories while they sat in the rain. They enjoyed eating all the biscuits while they waited for Alex and his father to return. Sophia was about to order more when a loud ruckus echoed throughout the house. She heard Alex shouting and the sound of breaking furniture.

Sophia told Henry to remain in the room and ordered a footman to stay with him, then she rushed along the hallway. She threw open the door to find Alex and Lord Delamont wrestling on the floor throwing punches as if they were adolescent boys.

"*Alexander*." Sophia's stern voice rose above them.

Sheffield looked up to see the fury on Sophia's face and realized he'd taken his anger too far. He stood, running a hand through his hair, looking down his nose at Delamont. The man didn't deserve any help from the floor. Sheffield walked away to pour himself a drink. After throwing the whiskey back in one shot he poured another, slowly sipping, watching Delamont rise to his feet.

Delamont arched an eyebrow at Sheffield. "Are you going to pour me one too?" Sheffield shrugged, pouring another glass. He held the drink toward him. Delamont tried to take a drink, but winced at the cut on his lip. Sheffield smirked in pleasure.

"What is the meaning of this outburst?" Sophia demanded.

"I am sorry, my dear, Lord Delamont needed my help on convincing him not to follow through with a private matter."

"Humph." Sophia knew there was more to this explanation.

"I apologize, Your Grace." Delamont sat his glass down and bowed to her. "I thank you for your kindness today. It was a pleasure to make your acquaintance."

Sophia watched Lord Delamont walk out of the room to collect his son. Their steps echoed in the hallway before they left. She turned to Alex and waited for him to explain himself.

"Don't look at me that way, my dear." Sheffield sighed, sliding into the chair near the fire. He held out his hand to her.

"Alex, I am most disappointed in your behavior. What prompted you to behave in that regard?"

"Come here love, and I will explain."

Sophia slid on his lap, placing soft kisses against the bruises forming on his jaw. She explained for him. "Delamont is the gentleman who Belle lost her heart to, and his little boy is the one who she visits with at the park."

"Yes."

"Whatever are we going to do?"

"We will do nothing, my dear wife."

"But—"

"But, nothing," Alex said firmly.

"Alex, my love—"

"No, Phee. Delamont destroyed Belle all those years ago, and I cannot stand by and watch him do it all over again. He does not deserve her."

"It is not for you to decide her fate."

"I made a promise to her, years ago, that I would protect her. Even from him. Delamont thinks because his wife is dead, he can pick up where he left off with Belle. She deserves better than that."

"She deserves for her heart to heal. Belle is lonely. When we spoke with her yesterday, we heard the yearning in her soul. Delamont is the only man that will make her feel complete. You cannot protect Belle from what her true heart desires."

Alex closed his eyes, trying to understand the rationale. No, he couldn't decide Belle's heart, only she could. He needed to warn Belle of Delamont's return and his connection to Henry before she discovered it first. With Lord Delamont's return to town, the rumor mill would spread the reasons for his return. As Belle's friend he needed to give her the news, and the truth of it.

"I need to tell her."

"*We* need to tell her."

Alex drew Sophia's lips under his. His wife's everlasting kindness seeped into his soul. He deepened the kiss, hoping that her goodness would somehow lead him to accept the fate of his friend. Sophia's kiss soothed him for the time being.

Chapter Four

Belle was livid. She followed Alice and Henry at a discreet distance.

She could stay silent no longer, even though she had only known the lad less than a week. In those few days, Belle had fallen under Henry's spell. She wouldn't have ventured out today, expect for the powerful urge to visit the park. She dressed warmly, wearing many layers. Belle had to fight a way through the fierce winds and the torrential rainfall to reach her destination. Ned had argued and insisted that she take a hackney, but Belle refused. She was in too much of a hurry to be stuck in a carriage that moved at a snail's pace. For some unknown reason, she knew Henry would be at the park all alone. And she wasn't mistaken.

When Belle hurried to the bench, she'd found Henry huddling in his sodden clothes, with not a stitch of a coat protecting him from the elements. He shivered from the chilly air, his teeth chattering when he tried to say hello. Belle rushed to Henry, trying to offer him shelter. His little body shook against hers. She pulled them to a gazebo, pulling off her coat and wrapping him up. Belle gathered him close, trying to heat his body, rocking them back and forth. Henry stared to cry. Belle soothed him, whispering gentle words to quiet his distress. She soon had Henry laughing, telling him stories about a sea captain and his pet monkey.

When Alice arrived from her tryst, Belle held nothing back. Belle lectured Alice on her indecency and said she would report Alice to Henry's father. Alice snidely replied that she knew Belle's real identity, and would make sure her employer knew too. If Belle were to report anything, she would be met with scorn. With a smug expression, Alice dragged Henry away.

Belle stood in shock. She had been so careful to hide her identity. She looked around to see if anybody had heard Alice's threats, even though the park was empty from the weather. If Alice had discovered the truth, who else knew? Still, Alice's threat wouldn't stop Belle from caring for Henry's welfare. Alice didn't scare Belle. She hadn't risen to her position without being threatened before. A mere governess wouldn't cower her.

So she followed Alice.

Belle knew where every member of the ton resided. She had made it her business. She even knew where Phillip supposedly lived—however, she'd never set foot in the townhouse and he never came to London anyway, not that she'd want to see him. Not once in all these years. Through the rise of temper she hadn't realized where her steps led now. Even when she knocked on the door, Belle didn't pause to consider the address. Then a disgruntled butler scrutinized her with disgust, distracting Belle further.

When Belle demanded to see the lord of the house, her tirade was loud enough to force the butler to lead Belle into a parlor near the rear, reluctantly offering a blanket. Belle was well aware that this was where the servants led unwanted guests. Then they would make you wait long enough so you either grew bored or angry. Where you would then decide to take your leave. Well, her anger would continue to grow, because Belle wasn't leaving this house until she met with Henry's father.

The butler shut the door and Belle paced back and forth across the parlor. With each trek across the rug, her anger *did* calm. If she confronted the lord in a fit, she wouldn't stand a chance to explain any concern for Henry's welfare. Belle paused when she caught her reflection in a mirror—

what the butler saw when he answered the door. A crazy woman with hair in a riot of curls sticking everywhere and clothes drenched. Belle tried pulling the material away from her body only to have it cling tighter. She looked like a vagabond. In the rush to get to the park, Belle didn't take much care with her appearance. Her only concern had been for Henry.

Belle sighed, stepping closer to the fireplace to dry off. However, the small fire didn't help to ward off the chills racking her body. Belle pulled the chair closer, wrapping the blanket tight. Soon the warmth of the room banished her chills and drowsiness settled over Belle. It didn't take long for her eyes to close and drift off to sleep. Her anger forgotten for a short while.

~~~~~

"Rosie, did you come to play?" A small hand poked at her shoulder, waking Belle from a dream. She opened her eyes to find Henry staring at her. She gazed around the unfamiliar room, then remembered. Belle had followed Alice to her employer, to confront the lord on the welfare of his son. The butler must have forgotten her. Belle kicked her legs out from underneath the blanket, stretching the kinks from her body, stiff from sleeping in a chair.

"No, love. Not this time. I came to speak with your father. Do you know where I may find him?" Belle ruffled Henry's hair.

"Papa is working in his study. He asked not to be disturbed. But he always reads me a bedtime story."

Belle looked out the window and noticed that darkness had descended. How long did she sleep? Ned would be worried. Belle needed to return home before he arranged a search party. Her conversation would have to wait. Now that Belle knew where Henry lived, she would return on the morrow to confront his father. She would dress as a proper lady who wouldn't allow the butler to deter her mission.

"Well, I do not wish to spoil your precious time with your papa. I will return tomorrow to speak with him and then perhaps he will give me permission to stay and play with you. Now, can you be a gentleman and show me to the door? I am afraid I must return home before my staff worries about me."

"Do you promise to return?"

"Yes, love," Belle reassured Henry, her heart strings tugging even more.

"All right."

Belle held out a hand and Henry slid his little palm against her. Moving down the hallway, he talked non-stop. Belle smiled fondly at him, then found it strange that they encountered no servants along the way.

"Henry, where are your servants?"

"Papa gave them the evening off. He detests when they hover. Papa has been in a snit ever since we visited his friend. But I do not think they were friends."

"Why do you say that?"

"The gentleman's wife was kind. Her name was Phee, and she fed me biscuits like you do. But her husband frowned a lot. Papa and the duke got into a brawl."

Phee? Did they visit Alexander and Sophia? Why? Who was Henry's father and what did he do to anger Sheffield?

"Henry, where are you?"

"Near the door, Papa. I am saying goodbye to Rosie. She promised to come back tomorrow to play."

Phillip's pace quickened when he heard Henry mention Rosie. What was Henry's friend doing alone at their home? Where were her parents? Phillip panicked, what should he do? He hoped Rosie could give him directions to home. Since he gave the servants the evening off, including the boy's governess, Philip held no clue on how to handle the situation. When Phillip rounded the corner he came to a halt. His son held the hand of a stunning creature. Even with her bedraggled appearance, she was a beauty. Was this the Rosie his son referred to? Why did it appear as if his son trusted this woman?

"Rosie?"

Belle was about to turn toward the footsteps but froze when she heard his voice. He'd only uttered her name and the flood of emotions rushed every memory through her soul. When Belle turned, the vision of Phillip standing before her caused her knees to buckle and she fell to the floor.

Phillip froze when she turned. His every fantasy stood in the foyer, holding Henry's hand. When she went limp, Phillip swept her in his arms, close to his chest, not once taking his eyes away. Their gazes collided, reflecting every memory shared. She lifted a hand to his cheek, whispering his name. Phillip closed his eyes at the gentle touch. When he opened them again, he saw tears slipping from her eyes. *He'd caused those.* What he wouldn't do to stop them. The pain reflected in the depth of her gaze invaded his soul, clinging to his heart. The ache that would never leave Phillip threatened to become overwhelming.

"My sweet Belle."

"No, Papa, her name is Rosie."

Phillip had forgotten all about his son. Rosalyn must have forgotten Henry too, because once she came out of her fog, she pressed at Phillip to let her go. With a reluctance, he set Rosalyn on her feet, keeping a hand on her waist, ready in case she fell again. He felt the slightly damp material and wondered why she was wet.

"Your friend from the park?" Phillip asked Henry.

"Yes, Rosie wanted to talk with you, but she has to go home now. She said she will return tomorrow and then we can play."

Phillip looked between his son and Rosalyn. Or Rosie, he should say. There was much he wanted to ask, but couldn't because of his son. Like hell, he wouldn't wait for her to return tomorrow. Judging from Rosalyn's expression she would never return. Obviously, Rosalyn held no knowledge that he was Henry's father. So that meant another reason for coming here. What he didn't understand was the unkempt appearance. Why did she appear as a beggar woman? Sheffield wouldn't allow it, if he was caring for her.

"Henry, please say your goodbyes to Rosie and get ready for bed. I will join you shortly. Perhaps Rosie will be so kind as to wait while I read a story and then we can have our discussion this evening. Then when she comes tomorrow, you will have longer to play."

Belle glared at Phillip. He used her affection for the boy to meet his demands. Phillip must have realized that Belle wouldn't refuse to avoid upsetting Henry. Well, Lord Delamont would learn he had been away for many years, and during that time Belle had learned how to manipulate with the best of them. Phillip may have thought he outsmarted her, but Belle was no longer that naïve girl he took advantage of—no, she was a woman in charge of her own destiny.

"Please say yes, Rosie. I will go to sleep right away and you will not have to wait for Papa long."

Belle knelt down to Henry's level. She planted a kiss on his cheek and wished him pleasant dreams. She also promised Henry to wait for his father.

Henry hugged her and ran up the stairs. She regarded him fondly, then turned toward Phillip. Belle willed herself to fight against every desire to throw herself at him—and not in anger.

"Do not leave, *Rosie*," Phillip said.

She didn't react to his command, except for nodding like an obedient child. Phillip headed for the stairs, then paused on the second step, turning back, not believing that she would still be there. When Rosalyn hadn't moved, he continued to Henry's room. Phillip planned to rush Henry's bedtime along, but Henry pleaded to being too tired to hear a story. Henry explained how he'd found Rosie in the back parlor, and how he spent the afternoon with Rosie at the park in the rain, and she'd given Henry a coat to stay warm.

It took an extreme effort for Phillip to remain calm. On the morrow it would appear he would need to be hiring not one but two new staff members. Phillip wouldn't tolerate insolence. Alice had abandoned Henry in the foul weather, and Rosalyn suffered disrespect at the hands of his butler. After assuring Henry he would return to Rosie, Phillip kissed him goodnight. He smiled, closing the door. It would appear Rosalyn's charm had ensnared his son.

Both of the Delamont men were enamored of a beauty who Phillip meant to capture and never let go of again.

Belle watched them hurriedly climb the stairs. She had two options. She could stay and inform Lord Delamont in no uncertain terms what he could do with his governess. Or she could leave. To stay in this house opened up so many vulnerabilities. Her emotions were too raw and seeing

Phillip again only opened up the old wounds. No, to keep her sanity, she must leave. If Belle stayed, she knew with one touch, one whispered word, she would be in his arms again. Lost to the emotions that only Phillip aroused. Then once he discovered the truth of her identity now, he would be revolted. Phillip would shield Henry, not wanting to tarnish his son's innocence. And he would be correct. Belle shouldn't have befriended the lad.

After Phillip reached the top of the stairs and entered Henry's bedroom, Belle snuck outside, escaping into the darkness. It was for the best. Now was the time to accept Sheffield's offer and leave town. Not forever, but long enough so Phillip would tire of looking for her and return to the country. Belle understood that she could never hold a respectful place in society because of her profession, and neither did she want that. She hated all the spitefulness that went on in the ton. No, Belle only wanted to live a quiet life. Perhaps a small cottage away from London. A decision she would make while away.

~~~~~

When Belle arrived home, it was to find Alex and Sophia waiting in the parlor. Sheffield paced back and forth, wearing a hole in the rug, while Sophia tried to soothe him. When Sophia noticed Belle in the doorway, she smiled sweetly, only this time it held sympathy too. There was only one man who could anger Sheffield to this degree, and that was Phillip.

Henry's story held true. Bruises covered Sheffield's face and they were already turning a variety of colors. Belle sighed. All in her honor. *Oh Alex, if you only knew*. Phillip only needed to take Belle in his arms and she would lose herself all over again. Belle didn't deserve Alex's protection. Belle knew in her heart that she would open herself to Phillip once more.

She looked at Sophia and saw the understanding in Sophia's gaze. Belle would have Sophia's support on whatever decision was made. Sophia nodded, relaying to Belle that she would take care of Alex.

"What did you do to incur Beckwith's wrath? I thought you two had made up and were now friends." Belle tried to tease Sheffield, but only ended up getting a scowl. Then Alex realized his reaction and he turned remorseful.

"'Tis was not with Beckwith."

"I know," Belle sighed.

"No, you do not understand the severity of the fight I had."

Belle came to Sheffield's side, sliding a hand over his cheek. She stared into his eyes, telling him how she understood what it all meant.

"You know."

Belle nodded. Sheffield pulled Belle into an embrace. And Belle let him, even with Sophia across the room. He had been her savior all those years ago and continued to still be the man she would run to with her troubles.

"Where have you been? Ned sent word that you did not return from your walk. We have been worried," Sheffield said.

"I followed Henry home. His governess, Alice, had me in such a temper that I didn't take into account my surroundings. Then the butler showed me into a parlor and they forgot me. I feel asleep in front of the fire. When Henry woke me, I made an excuse to leave. Right before I walked out the door, Phillip spoke my name." Her voice caught.

Sophia came over and led Belle to the sofa. She was well aware that Belle would be emotional from seeing Lord Delamont for the first time in this many years.

"What happened?" Sophia asked

Belle laughed, "I almost fainted, and he caught me."

"If he so much as went any further than that, I will—" Sheffield growled.

"No, you will not." Sophia and Belle said together.

"Yes, I will."

Both women stared him down.

"Nothing happened, Henry was present. Phillip thought he'd persuaded me to stay, using his son as an excuse. I agreed like the meek girl I used to be." Belle laughed wryly. "Then once they continued to Henry's room, I left."

She rose and paced the floor in the same path Sheffield had been stalking.

"Does Phillip believe me to be that same trusting girl? He thought I would follow through on any request he made."

Sheffield smiled. This was Belle. No, she would not be succumbing to Delamont's charm. He'd worried for nothing.

Sophia watched her husband's smug smile, shaking her head in disbelief of the situation. Alex meant well, but he would be sorely disappointed once Belle gave into her emotions toward Lord Delamont— and she would. As much as Belle angrily spouted off on the nerve of the man, Sophia saw the sexual awakening of Belle. Sophia noticed how Belle glowed, and the warm blush stealing across Belle's cheeks each time she mentioned Lord Delamont's name.

"Sheffield, is the offer of your home on the coast still available?"

"Anything for you, Belle."

"I believe I need some time away. Will you look after my business? I realize how unorthodox it would be for a duke to run a brothel, but I trust no one but you."

"Leave it to me and Wilde, and with Beckwith and Holdenburg's help your establishment will run smoothly. Each of us will take a night while you are away and see that no trouble occurs. I will go talk to Ned now. Is there anything else I can help you with, Belle?"

"No, you have helped me more than enough. I can never repay you for your generosity."

"I think we are even, my dear. If it were not for you, I would not have found the happiness I share with Sophia. I only wish you the same. Lord Delamont is not the one to bring you that happiness though."

"Alex," Sophia warned.

"I will let this rest for now. But once you return, he will discover the truth of your status in society. Can you handle how he will react?"

"It does not matter anymore. I understood the repercussions the day I asked for your help. Our relationship finished on that fateful afternoon years ago, when I waited for him. Instead of sharing the wonderful news of the babe I carried, he told me of his upcoming nuptials. No, Lord Delamont means nothing to me. He is only the father to the young boy I met and fell in love with. I will speak to Phillip one day, but I cannot right now."

"Very well, I will make arrangements with Ned."

Once Sheffield left, Belle turned to Sophia, knowing that she had much to say, but not with Alex present.

"All the same feelings are there, are they not?"

"Aye."

"Are you running from him, or those feelings?"

"They are the same, are they not?"

"Perhaps."

Belle realized that Sophia was waiting to hear more. How could she explain the fear that if she stayed, Belle could never leave him again? That she would accept whatever Phillip offered. If the only option he extended was for Belle to warm his bed at night, then Belle would do so with an eagerness that resembled what she witnessed from her girls.

"There are no words to describe how he makes me feel. How can I describe an emotion that rips the very soul from my body?"

"You cannot, my dear. I know that only too well."

"Yes, you do, don't you?"

"What about Henry?"

"Can you deliver a message to him? That I had to leave town, but I will visit him soon at the park?"

"Yes, I can do that. I will do better than that. I shall visit him at the park until you return."

"Thank you, Sophia, your friendship in my time of need means more than I can say."

"I do not think Lord Delamont is the type of gentleman to keep his distance for very long."

"He is not. He was relentless when he first captured my heart. These lost years have only made him more so. And I know my heart cannot resist him."

"I understand."

"Alex will be furious."

"Alex will come to understand in time."

Sophia would make him see reason. It was not too long ago that Alex sought forgiveness. Sophia had opened her heart to Alex again, just as Belle would for Lord Delamont.

Chapter Five

Sheffield's butler led Delamont into Sheffield's study immediately upon his arrival. It was as if Sheffield expected him. A room full of protectors waited for him when he entered. Every man wore an expression of hatred. They were here for Rosalyn, but not one of these men would succeed. Delamont would find a way around them to reach her.

When Delamont came downstairs, that evening in his house, he found that Rosalyn had fled after all. He'd used Henry to blackmail her into staying and her meek reply fooled him into believing that she would. Delamont had sensed a strong, independent woman who didn't let a mere man push her around. No, she was a goddess, and they were all in her domain. Delamont had wanted to search for Rosalyn, but with no staff had to stay at home.

Throughout the night he paced his house like a tiger wanting to go after its prey. He watched the sunset strike against the sky, the bright rays raking across his bloodshot eyes. When the butler arrived to take over his duties, Delamont fired him on the spot. It was a message to rest of his staff that he wouldn't tolerate any form of disrespect toward his guests. Then he went up to Henry's room, telling him to wait in the dining room where they would eat breakfast together. With Henry downstairs, Delamont fired Alice.

Then he received a letter from Sophia informing Phillip that she was passing along a message from a friend, and it explained in detail on how the friendship between Rosie and Henry came to be. It would appear his governess used the outings to have secret trysts with the stable hand at the mews adjacent to the park. His fury grew. Alice had neglected Henry for her own pleasure. If it weren't for Rosalyn's attention, Phillip imagined what could have befallen his son. He ordered the housekeeper to watch over Alice's departure.

But not before the governess had her say too.

"You think to judge me? Well, let me tell you that the lady Rosie your boy speaks so fondly of is nothing more than a whore. She spreads her thighs in a house near Covent Gardens. She is even the madame. Rosie? Hah! More like Madame Bellerose. Listen for her name; gentlemen whisper it all around London. So do not think your boy spends time with an innocent lady." Alice took much glee in revealing this.

He'd heard of Madame Bellerose. Hell, most of his acquaintances since coming to town spoken of the brothel, giving advice on where to find discreet pleasure since the passing of his wife. Did what Alice say hold any truth? He knew Rosalyn had taken up with Sheffield when he left, and Sheffield didn't deny having her for his mistress. But a brothel owner? No, not Rosalyn. She wouldn't take that special name and use it for a shameful profession.

"Sheffield, Wildeburg, Beckwith," he acknowledged the men. "I am afraid we have not been introduced yet?" He held out his hand to the other gentleman. However, his gesture was returned with a look of disgust.

Sheffield laughed, slapping the man on the back. "This here is Holdenburg. To most of the ton, he is a womanizing drunk, and a card shark who will strip your fortunes bare."

"I am no longer a womanizer. Nor do I drink as before."

"Yes, you are correct. All due to the lovely Kathleen. You are as much of a changed man as the rest in this room. All except for the one who stands before us. He is more of a scoundrel than all of us together."

"Cut the crap, Sheffield. Where can I find her?"

"Find whom?"

"You know damn well who I seek. You and none of these men will stop me from finding her."

"Belle does not wish to be found," growled Beckwith.

"Rosalyn is none of your concern, but mine," Delamont said.

"Actually Belle is all of our concerns. We will do what we have to, to protect her from the likes of you," Wildeburg said.

"I do not wish to hurt her," Delamont sighed. "I only wish to speak to Rosalyn."

"She goes by Belle," Holdenburg interrupted.

"That name is not meant for anybody else to use, but me."

"You do not matter in Belle's life anymore, Delamont," Sheffield taunted.

"That is not for you to say, only for her. I am tired of this game we are playing. Where the hell is she?" Delamont's voice had risen.

"It's none of your damn business." Sheffield advanced on Delamont, ready to pound on him again.

Wilde stepped between the two again.

"Still playing the peacemaker I see, Wildeburg," Delamont goaded.

"Do you want me to step aside? Because if I do, it will not only be at the hands of Sheffield you would have to defend yourself, but every man in this room."

"Let me guess, after Sheffield finished with Rosalyn, the rest of you used her to seek your pleasure?"

Wilde stepped back. The fool hadn't learned when to keep his mouth shut.

Delamont deserved every punch that came his way, Wilde himself even took pleasure at the right hook he gave Delamont. It would appear the gentleman needed lessons on what was required to be called a gentleman. Once Beckwith pounded on him a few times, Holdenburg pulled his brother-in-law away. Wilde thought Delamont had had enough, but Holdenburg took his fists to the man too. The whole time Sheffield stood back and never wiped the satisfied smirk from his face. Wilde shook his head. He should have known Sheffield baited Delamont to make his foolish comments. Sheffield knew more than anybody what it took to set Delamont off. Usually Wilde could deflect Sheffield's comments and keep the peace. But with his own investment in Belle's happiness, he was blinded to Sheffield's ploy. Wilde only saw red that this man was the reason Belle kept her heart frozen all these years. He himself had tried many times to unfreeze her. Wilde had to admit, he would have been more than willing to slip between her thighs at one time. That was before he fell in love with Sidney. But Belle always refused him before things went too far. The most they shared were a few kisses. Their friendship meant more to Wilde than the pleasure of her body. A pleasure Belle only wanted to share with one man—and that man stood before him now. Nay, more like slumped in a chair.

Wilde winced when the door flew open and their wives invaded the room, his own leading the pack. When they noticed the beaten Lord Delamont, each man received a scolding from their wife.

While the women shouted their dismay, Delamont watched in disbelief. Each woman was shockingly beautiful in their own right. They were defending him, and once each woman finished with their husband, they bombarded Delamont about his welfare. When he raised his eyes, Sheffield shrugged at him, no longer wearing a smirk of satisfaction at Delamont's beating. Sheffield poured himself and the rest of the men a drink, excluding Delamont. But Sophia frowned and poured Delamont a drink too, bringing it to him.

"Lord Delamont, it would appear that you have angered our husbands. I can only assume it was because you made a derogatory comment about Belle that I am sure my husband provoked you into saying. Am I right?" Sophia asked.

Delamont didn't answer. He couldn't, because she stood correct. He had disrespected Rosalyn and had no excuse except for plain old-fashioned jealousy. If he said yes, it wouldn't play him in a good light with Sheffield. No, he wouldn't resort to childhood antics of tattle-telling. Delamont would take his beating as a man who deserved it, no less.

The brunette next to Sophia muttered, "Sophia, he will not admit to that. It would make him weak to the other men. You are not his mother."

"Yes, Sidney is correct. However, I am sure one of our husbands will admit to what transpired here." The redhead looked pointedly at Beckwith.

"Dallis, he deserved every punch. You would have too, if you heard the words he spoke of Belle."

Dallis shook her head, causing the dark-haired beauty to laugh at Beckwith. When Beckwith scowled, Holdenburg put a protective arm around the chit. Delamont's head spun from all the conversations echoing around the study. His skull pounded from the beating and the mindless chit-chat. He was still no closer to discovering Rosalyn's whereabouts.

It was when the dark-haired beauty spoke that he stilled.

"Since you are new to town, you do not understand how your words toward Belle not only would have hurt her feelings, if she heard them, but how they have hurt every individual in this room." The young lady's speech seemed to calm everyone, bringing murmurs of agreement.

"How would my words affect everyone in this room, my lady?"

"It's Kathleen, my lord. Because if it were not for Belle, then all of our marriages would never have come to be."

"Belle has been instrumental in helping with my matchmaking attempts for us to have the happy unions we have today," said Sidney.

"Not now, Sidney," they all moaned good-naturedly.

"Matchmaking?" Delamont became more confused.

"Excuse our friend Sidney. She gets overly excited when discussing her matchmaking attempts. We like to humor her," Dallis quipped.

"You girls encourage her," Wilde moaned.

Everybody laughed. It would appear to Delamont that this was a tight knit of friends and they had included Belle into their fold. Never had he felt like more of an outsider than right now. At one time, Sheffield and he had been close friends. One horrific incident in his life caused him to lose that friendship along with the love of his life.

"I would enjoy hearing of how Belle was instrumental in your relationships, but I must return to my son. I promised him we would visit his favorite park."

"Find another park, Delamont," Sheffield demanded.

"I will not, Sheffield. Especially since she might appear there at any time."

Wilde tried to explain, "Do not take away her sanctuary. She goes there to escape and your very presence will invade her privacy."

"I mean her no harm."

"You returning to London causes harm that Belle may never recover from. You were not there the last time. Your abandonment destroyed her.

Every person in this room will make sure that you do not get the chance to again," threatened Sheffield.

Delamont rose and left without saying a word. Between the hostile looks from the gentleman and pitying stares from the ladies, he'd had enough. None of these couples would keep him from the woman he loved. Delamont had wronged Rosalyn, but he planned on making things right.

~~~~~

"Do you think he took our threats seriously?" Holdenburg asked.

"No, my dear he did not," Kathleen replied, squeezing his hand on her shoulder.

"No, he is a man determined to win his love," Sidney sighed.

Every set of eyes turned on Sidney at once. They knew what that sigh meant and what it would lead to. Trouble. Nothing but trouble.

"My dear, this is one that you must sit out on," Wilde said.

"Why?" This came from Dallis, not Sidney.

"Yes, why?" asked Sophia. Sophia and Sidney were best friends and whenever Sidney had a plan, Sophia always got involved.

"Because I say so," Sheffield said.

All the women laughed at Sheffield's arrogant tone. When Sophia smiled his way, Sheffield lost his argument. At one time, everybody would obey him. Since he'd married Sophia, he had become a pushover whenever she crooked her finger.

He said wearily, "Very well, but only on one condition."

They all nodded.

"If at any time Belle no longer wishes for his attention, each one of you will abide by her wishes. Agreed?"

"Agreed," Sophia answered for all of them. "Ladies, would you care to take a stroll with me? I am sure the gentlemen have business to discuss. It is a fine day."

When the ladies kissed their husbands goodbye, Sheffield knew something was already afoot. While Sophia and Sidney often took long walks, the entire group of ladies together rarely did.

What did his wife have planned now?

~~~~~

Belle rested on her usual bench, talking with Claire and holding the babe, the bag of biscuits next to her. The older children played nearby. The only child missing was Henry. Belle had hoped to see him before she left town. She wanted to reassure Henry that she wasn't abandoning him. Sophia had promised to visit the park while Belle was away and explain things to Henry, but it wasn't the same.

"Well lookie there, Rosie, at the grand ladies coming our way. Are they not beautiful and their dresses so lovely?" Claire spoke in awe.

Oh no. What were they doing here?

Belle took a risk coming here today after what Alice had said. But when Claire sat down and laid the babe in her arms, Belle felt confident her secret was safe. Now, how would she explain any relationship with these aristocratic friends to anybody at the park? When the ladies stopped in front of the bench with determination on their faces, Belle feared the gig was up. Then Sophia surprised her.

"Hello, Rosie. We missed you at our meeting for the Ladies of Mayfair's Homeless Children's Fund."

"I apologize for my absence since you so gracefully extended an invitation to join your organization. I wanted to visit the park before I left town for a few days."

"You are leaving town?" Claire asked in dismay. Belle knew Claire had become dependent on these visits, because it provided a break from the children. Belle would fuss over the babe while the other children played, and Claire could take a few moments for herself and relax.

"Only for a few days, Claire. I will return shortly."

"Oh." Claire's despair was so evident to the other ladies that Belle felt the need to explain after she made introductions.

"This is my friend, Claire. We meet in the park daily. While her children play, I get to spoil the babe while Claire has some time for herself."

"Oh, you poor dear, I only have one child, I cannot even imagine three," said Dallis.

"Yes, well, Rosie eases those burdens with a few kind words every day," Claire nervously explained.

"Yes, Rosie is a kind friend. Perhaps you would not mind our company while she is away?" Sophia asked.

"Oh, I could not impose on you grand ladies."

"We are only ladies, just like you. There is nothing grand about us. Only our offer of friendship," said Kathleen.

Before Belle could stop them, Sophia grabbed the babe out of her arms and fussed over him. Then they passed the infant between each of them. Each lady charmed Claire into confiding her troubles with them. Belle shook her head at their interference and walked away a short distance where she stood, watching them.

"Your friends are a force of nature."

"Yes, they are." Belle didn't need to turn around to know who stood behind. She had sensed Phillip was near. Also, Sidney had the look of matchmaking written all over her face.

"Belle, will you please turn around? I only wish a few words for now."

"For now? What about later?"

"That will be entirely your decision to make."

Before Belle turned around, she noticed Henry playing with his group of friends. He waved with his toothy grin. Belle waved back.

"He had hoped you would be here."

Belle turned. "And you?"

"Yes, and me too." He lifted a hand to brush across her cheek.

"Don't," Belle said, stepping back.

Phillip dropped his hand. It would be inappropriate to touch her in public. But the temptation prompted the attempt.

"Belle."

"At the park, I go by Rosie, so please address me in that form. I would prefer not to answer to questions of a different name."

"Rosie."

Before Belle could respond, the children descended on them begging for their treat. She smiled fondly at them. She told Nicholas to gather the sack from the bench. He tore off and returned with it. Belle rewarded each child with a biscuit caked with icing. They ran and sat near the tree, eating the delicious treat. Before Henry sat down he kicked the ball and it rolled into the bushes. Belle laughed, telling him to sit and she would retrieve the ball.

Phillip saw their exchange and gazed adoringly at Belle—or Rosie, as she wished to be called. Which confused him even more because the ladies at Sheffield's referred to her as Belle. Why both names? What was the hidden meaning in each? And why did she no longer call herself Rosalyn?

When Belle disappeared into the shrubbery to retrieve the ball, Phillip followed. He glanced around to make sure of their privacy. When his gaze encountered Sophia's, she winked. Did the duchess actually approve? He called out Rosie's name and when he found her, the image seared into his mind. She was bent over and pulling the ball away from the bushes. Her hips wiggled. What may have been an innocent act brought memories of Rosalyn naked as he took her from behind. His Belle had always enjoyed exploring different positions in their lovemaking. Phillip remembered the curve of her backside when his hand fondly stroked her fires, and her moans when she came undone in his arms. Her breasts were heavy when he stroked her nipples into tight buds.

Each memory came alive—and could be blamed for what he did next.

When Belle pulled the ball loose, she turned to find Phillip standing right behind her. His intense stare drugged her senses. The ball was dropped, forgotten, when he drew her into his arms. Every second of the last seven years without him drifted away with the wind. His mouth descended and ravished every last breath. Phillip's grip tightened as their kiss consumed each other. Belle wanted to cry from the pleasure. She clung to him, needing to ease the ache of loneliness. Belle had never forgotten Phillip, no matter how she tried to convince her heart. Something she still tried to deny.

Phillip kissed Belle's lips like a man starved for only one woman—for Belle. Never before had there been a need this strong to be fulfilled. He'd had yearned for an eternity to taste Belle's lips again. But it wouldn't be enough. It would never be enough. When she clung to him, he knew that Belle remembered and wanted to share the same passion again.

He dragged his lips away and stared deep in her eyes. Phillips saw his own need reflected back. Belle was filled with the same desire. But Phillip also saw the wariness and didn't want to frighten her away. He ran his thumb across the bottom of her swollen lip. Belle closed her eyes at this touch.

Their need sizzled in the air, drawing their bodies closer. Phillip held Belle, tucking her head underneath his chin while they caught their breath. Belle stepped away after a time, and when Phillip reached to cup her cheek, she allowed him.

"I will wait for the rest of my life for the second that you forgive me. My heart aches for that day."

Belle turned and walked away from Phillip. She had no reply to something that Belle didn't know if she ever could do. He asked too much.

Phillip followed Belle out of the woods, carrying the ball under his arm. She was kneeling in front of Henry. When they were finished talking, she held her arms out for him. Henry snuggled into the embrace as if it were the most natural thing in the world. She placed a kiss on his cheek and walked over to her friends. Belle spoke to the lady on the bench, and Sophia and the others before she left. He started to follow, throwing the ball to Henry, but the ladies inadvertently stepped into his path. Without being a brute and plowing through them, he walked behind their slow pace and endless chatter. Once they reached the gate, he searched for the direction Belle had gone. He stopped and glanced around. There was no sign. It was as if she'd disappeared into thin air. When Phillip turned a puzzled gaze to her friends, they smiled their sympathy.

It had been deliberate, making sure that he couldn't follow her home. Once again Belle was lost to him.

Chapter Six

Phillip watched his son play with his friends. He had come to enjoy these daily outings Every day they would walk to the park. Each day hoping to see Belle. But there had been no sign of her. Henry explained to Phillip on the first day that Rosie was out of town. However, that didn't stop Phillip from wishing she would return soon. Their time spent walking back and forth from the park was filled with memorable conversations. It was an hour carved out of his busy day, precious time with Henry. Henry would run and play with his friends, and Phillip would then spend time becoming better acquainted with Belle's lady friends.

While she was away, each would take a turn visiting the park and help Claire. Belle's friends were from two different classes of life. Like Belle, they never let their status in the ton influence their behavior towards the working class that visited the park. They would hold Claire's babe and share stories of Belle. Never once revealing who Belle was. They always referred to her as Rosie. None of their tales surprised him. Belle was a generous soul who wanted to help anyone with their troubles. They even kept to Belle's tradition and brought treats for the children.

However, today Phillip grew impatient for Belle's return.

"Has she come home?"

"No," Sophia replied, giving him another look of pity. He was tired of receiving them.

"Not that you would share the information with me, if she did return."

"My answer would surprise you, Lord Delamont."

Phillip turned at her murmured response. Claire had left with the children, and Sophia kept him company when Henry found another child to play with.

"I thought you held the same opinion as your husband."

Sophia laughed. "Sheffield and I do not agree on many subjects. Especially this one. But then you must understand, Lord Delamont, that when you left Belle all those years ago, he was the one to pick up the pieces."

"So you will inform me when Belle returns?"

"Perhaps." Sophia shrugged, giving him a wink.

"Does Sheffield realize how lucky he is to have you?"

"Oh, yes. And if he forgets, I make it a point to remind him."

Phillip laughed at the lucky bastard.

Henry ran over and Phillip helped Sophia from the bench. Henry slipped a hand inside her palm and they walked along the path. They escorted Sophia to her house safely before they made their own way home. Phillip knew Belle would return to them soon. He only had to show a little more patience.

~~~~~

Belle walked along the beach, enjoying the mist spraying around her legs. Even though it was highly improper for a lady to show her ankles, Belle didn't have to worry. Sheffield's estate contained a private stretch of sand. While most of the time she liked to surround herself with people, these last few days Belle enjoyed the tranquility of being alone. Her toes dug into the grainy sand. Belle's thoughts played over the decisions she needed to make before returning. Even though her heart had already made its choice. She'd been undecided before the kiss in the park. However, after the kiss, returning to Phillip's arms became inevitable. Belle's heart no longer wanted to fight through the pain or cared if Phillip would hurt her again. No, Belle's heart ached to be with Phillip.

Belle sunk to the beach. Her fingers trailed through the sand and she watched the waves of the North Sea. A vast body of water floating peacefully at the moment. However, at one touch of a storm, it would become a misery. So much like how she felt at the moment. Belle found a sense of peace in the time away, but her emotions hovered close to the surface, because a storm was near. Would she be in misery, if she allowed Philip back into her life? Or would their relationship float peacefully?

Questions. Over the course of the last few days, Belle had asked herself many, and she still held no answers. She needed to return and seek answers from Phillip. Since she had already come to the conclusion of what her heart had decided, Belle wanted Phillip any way she could have him. Now, it was left to Phillip to decide if he truly wanted her.

Chapter Seven

Belle strolled into her office, at peace with herself and with a sense of direction. The time away had brought a spring to her step. All the colors looked brighter, and the conversations with staff took on a new vibrancy. Even the scowl on Sheffield's face when he informed Belle of what happened at the club while she was away didn't deter her bliss. When his scowl deepened at her happiness, Belle only smiled more.

"You're going to forgive him, aren't you?"

"Thank you for your help, Sheffield, and the use of your home. One day I shall repay your kindness."

Sheffield sighed. "You already have, my dear. You have my support for your future and my arms are always open if you find a reason to need them again."

Belle kissed his cheek. "Give Phee my love."

Belle slipped inside the bedroom to change. Her fingers slid over the sensuous garments, trying to decide what to wear. When one hand paused over a daring violet creation, she'd found her choice. Belle slipped the dress over her curves, smiling in the mirror at the image. The plunging neckline hugged her breasts, pushing them tight together. She turned to the side, moving one leg back and forth to see how much of the slit showed. Belle decided to wear her hair down this evening. The long luxurious red curls draped along her back. She drew a few strands near her breasts. That way, when she walked, they would tease every gentleman in the club with a temptation to bed her. Belle enjoyed the power of her sexuality. It built her confidence—and bank account. She would offer them a few teasing words, then convince them to instead sample the delights from one of the girls above stairs. And every time, they would moan their disappointment, but become entranced with her beauties.

This evening she wanted to bring every one of them to their knees and this dress would succeed in that. She wanted it whispered on every gentleman's lips that she had returned to London. Before long Lord Delamont would come calling. No man had ever resisted trying to win her hand, and he would be no different. While the gossip mill rumored that Phillip didn't visit brothels, he did enjoy a high-stake game of cards. The only place to find a game with a deep pot in London was at The Wager.

Belle walked into the salon and welcomed some gentlemen wishing to seek a room above stairs. She flirted with them, making them feel desired. Then she moved on to the card room and saw to the player's comforts. Belle made the rounds, prompting the rumors to begin. These same men would make their appearance at events throughout the evening and return later seeking their pleasures.

"Welcome back, Belle. You are looking extremely dangerous this evening."

"It is good to be home, Ned. Thank you for helping Sheffield while I was away. Do we have any new customers?" She ignored his comment about her appearance. She would not divulge who she dressed for.

"None."

"If there is, please inform me immediately."

"Will do, boss."

Belle sensed that Phillip would seek membership this evening. When he did, she would be ready for him. Their affair would be on her terms, not his.

~~~~~

Phillip's gaze drifted across the ballroom, searching for Rosalyn. But she wasn't here. She would never be here. Sophia explained that Rosalyn didn't frequent balls or any events the ton held. Sophia didn't go into detail, but Phillip thought there was more to the explanation.

"Madame Bellerose has made a return and looks even more exquisite than ever."

"She made my mouth water in the dress she wore. I wish she would open her bedroom to the ton. But she only teases us with her body."

"To drink from those breasts, mmm. If I were a cheating man, she would be the woman to bed. Those long legs and beautiful mane of red hair. To hold that hair while she pleasured me brings me to my knees from just imagining."

"However, you and no man will ever hold that privilege."

Phillip listened to the private conversation behind him. The talk disgusted him. Their crude behavior made him want to slug them. They may have been talking about a harlot, but she was also a woman that had feelings. No woman, whatever her profession may be, deserved to be spoken of in that way.

Phillip was trapped behind the columns and had to endure listening to their conversation. If he walked out, they would know he had eavesdropped. So, instead he listened as they spoke of Madame Bellerose and her place of business. The brothel included a gaming hell and a boxing ring. Her empire was so exclusive that there were only two ways to gain entry. She had to approve your membership either by making you a guest, or you had to have another member sponsor you. This way it kept out the usual riff-raff of unwanted players. Only the members of the ton who could gamble to the limits were allowed access at the tables. You must specify what services you sought at the interview process. She approved every membership personally. The only way to seek entry was a token that represented your pleasure.

The more he listened to them, the more Alice Timmon's comments made him wonder if there *was* a connection between Rosalyn and Madame Bellerose. Did Alice stand correctly on Belle's true identity? Or were they words of a fired servant seeking revenge? The gentlemen's conversation mentioned that Madame Bellerose had returned to town. Rosalyn had left town for a few days. Sheffield and her friends referred to her as Belle. However, her friends from the park called her Rosie. Each time he had seen Rosalyn, she dressed simple. If she were a Madame, her attire would be flashy. His confusion grew. Either way, he wanted answers.

While Phillip would never seek the pleasures found in a brothel, he was in the mood for a friendly game of cards. Anything to get his mind off Rosalyn. Stalking her old haunts had turned him into an obsessed man. His behavior even to himself was unsettling. Phillip decided to walk out from behind the columns and into the middle of their conversation. One of the lords wanted his support on a new bill in Parliament. They had been calling on him, seeking his vote for over a week now. He could invite Phillip to Madame Bellerose's establishment, then Phillip could discover the truth.

"Gentleman, I am afraid that I had overheard your private conversation."

"Nothing is too private, Lord Delamont, when it concerns the delectable Belle." Lord Farwick slapped Phillip on the shoulder.

"Belle?"

"Ah, yes I keep forgetting you are new to town. Madame Bellerose, to be exact. An amazing creature you must meet."

"She sounds delightful. But what I crave is a game of high-stakes cards. Do you know where I might find one?"

"You must come with us to Belle's. Her gaming hell, The Wager, is the only place you will find a good game. We are returning there shortly. We have only made an appearance to appease our wives before we took our pleasures elsewhere this evening."

Phillip laughed along with their atrocious behavior, wanting to fit in with the outlandish antics. Disgust settled within him as he agreed to their invitation. Phillip would pay this establishment a visit. He would see if Rosalyn *was* the notorious Madame Bellerose. After his foolish thoughts were laid to rest, he would spend a few hours forgetting Rosalyn. Perhaps, after a few drinks, she would become a distant memory until tomorrow morning. Where once again he would take the daily stroll with his son, hoping beyond all hope for a chance to see Rosalyn's smiling face.

~~~~~

"Belle, we have a gentleman requesting membership. Do you want him to return another evening?"

Belle sighed. Her back ached from sitting at the desk the last few hours. She had worked the floor earlier in the evening appeasing her guests, then headed to the office to do paperwork. Important clientele were attending a ball the ton had thrown and would fill the club later.

"No, Ned. A break would do nicely. Please show him to the parlor adjoining my bedroom. After the interview, I think I will rest before the rush begins. Who is sponsoring him?"

"Lord Farwick."

Belle grimaced, for she secretly detested Lord Farwick. The man was a reprobate. He'd tried many attempts to seduce her. Lord Farwick had two marks against him, and with one more she could revoke his membership. If the members made minor infractions that harmed nobody, she would place a mark against their account. Once they reached three, she would revoke their token and they could never return. If any of their actions caused harm to any girl, servant, or other member of her club, Belle would have them removed immediately.

Ned was called away before Belle could ask about the identity of the newcomer. It didn't matter, she would soon discover for herself.

Belle paused in the doorway to the parlor and regarded who the gentleman might be. She kept the door open in case she needed to call the guard, if she didn't feel safe. Belle saw Phillip standing across the room with his back to the door, examining the book shelves. She whispered to the guard that she would not need his services, and closed the door.

Phillip turned at the click of the lock. He had been told Madame Bellerose would conduct the interview in a private parlor. A guard delivered him to a room he hadn't expected. Madame Bellerose's bookshelves had drawn him closer. His fingers trailed over the tomes, reading the titles. An intellectual display of books, many of them first editions that he could never acquire. How had this brothel owner attained them? When Phillip turned, his disbelief kept him rooted to his spot.

Belle saw the surprise in Phillip's eyes as she leaned against the door. The mystery man needed no introduction. She knew him on a level of no other. Belle's intuition on seeing him this evening had come true. Even when the evening grew late, the sense held strong.

However, she realized Phillip hadn't connected Rosalyn, Rosie, and Belle together before now.

Phillip wanted to drop to his knees and worship the creature cascaded in violet. The shock lasted for the briefest of moments before everything clicked into place. Rosalyn, Rosie, Belle, all made perfect sense now. The need to keep her identity a secret at the park. The reason she would never be in attendance at any event within the ton. Rosalyn *was* Madame Bellerose. And if the rumors were true, then Belle bedded no man. Rosalyn was as pure today as she was when he left her, except for Sheffield. Phillip wouldn't blame Rosalyn for Sheffield. To be fair, he'd had Julia's companionship all those years, so he couldn't fault Rosalyn for not wanting to be alone.

The bastards from the ball didn't do her justice. Their meager compliments paled in comparison. The violet creation hugged every curve. The plunging neckline begged for his tongue to trace the path of what she kept hidden. Phillip wanted to slide his hand up the slit of the dress to see if she wore anything beneath. But he already knew that Belle didn't. Phillip longed to strip away the dress and see her hair spread out on the bed, entangling between their bodies. The whisper of soft curls caressing him.

Belle watched the desire enflame Phillip. His passion filled her senses. Now he knew the truth. But instead of the revulsion she expected to see, she only saw his need. He needed her as much as she needed him. Her heart beat faster at the primal sensation. Should she open the door to the private chamber? Or conduct the interview for membership into the club? For all Belle knew, Phillip might want the use of one of her girls for the evening. A younger, more delectable woman, not an aging brothel owner.

Phillip watched the indecision cross Belle's face. He needed to stop whatever doubts she held. He didn't want Belle to let common sense to take hold. No, he needed to show how they were meant for each other. He needed to love her.

He advanced before Belle drew another breath. She'd opened her mouth to address him when his lips crushed to hers, kissing with a passion that only they shared. Phillip invaded all rational thought, only making her feel. To experience every wonder he brought to life. Not one stroke of his fingers, or touch of his lips went unnoticed. When his kiss softened to a slow caress, Belle moaned and melted in his arms.

Home. She was finally home.

Phillip raised his head at the moan, picking her up. She pointed to a door. No words needed to be spoken for what they both desired. He opened the door and strode through to the bedroom—a place no man had entered. He would be the first. And only.

He lowered her to the floor and then knelt at her feet. Belle ran fingers through his hair, urging him to look up. His vulnerability stopped him. It was stronger than from their time long ago. Probably because he had been a confident young man, sure of his destiny. When he'd had to let her go, he accepted his fate, although Phillip had never let go of his *dream* that one day she might be his again. Now that Belle stood before him, his dream a reality, he felt a humility that he didn't quite understand.

Belle shivered when Phillip's hand slid up the length of her leg. The soft caress seeped into her. When his fingers grazed the inside of her thigh, Belle's moan echoed around them. Phillip finally looked into her eyes when his fingers slid against her curls, sinking into wetness. He slid in deeper, bringing pleasure. Each stroke of his finger and whispered kiss had Belle trembling. When Phillip lifted her leg over his shoulder and replaced his finger with his tongue, Belle became lost in a sensation she hoped never to return from. Each glide of his touch created a need that only grew stronger. When Phillip's mouth grew bolder and she became undone, Belle cried out his name.

The sweet flavor of Belle on his lips weakened Phillip's knees. But the need to savor the rest of her body had him rising from her sweet heaven. His tongue traced the crest along her breasts, teasing him.

Belle's breasts ached for Phillip to hold. For him to take her buds into his mouth while he sucked them tight. How she had yearned for him all these years. Lost in desire, she didn't realize Phillip had slid the dress away and she stood before him naked. His passion shook Belle to the core. He lifted her breasts, holding them in the palms of his hands, and dipped his head to suck her nipples. Phillip's mouth took possession, leaving not one part of her untouched. Belle denied herself touching Phillip while he worshipped her body. Not that she didn't want to—it was because she refused herself. If Belle gave into her desires, then she would be forever lost. So, she held herself back.

Phillip understood why Belle didn't speak. For if she spoke, he would hear her vulnerability. She would feel like she had lost control. However, Belle was mistaken, she was the one who held all the power.

Phillip laid Belle across the bed, her hair flaring out over the bed sheets, fulfilling his fantasy. Phillip quickly discarded his clothing before Belle changed her mind. Phillip lay next to her on the bed and gathered her in his arms. Belle lifted her head and Phillip devoured her mouth in a kiss, drugging their senses with a passion needing to be satisfied.

Belle took control of the kiss. She wanted to make Phillip just as mindless with desire. She wanted to ingrain herself to where he would never forget her again.

Because they would have nothing more than this night.

It was impossible. They were from two different worlds. Even in the past they'd walked separate paths. Back then, because of her status in society, they could have made it work. Now, she would always be known as the brothel owner. She refused to bring shame onto Phillip and Henry like that.

Belle thought she could lie there, allow Phillip to make love to her, and not give any part of herself to him. But she was wrong. Belle craved to touch Phillip, to trace her lips across his skin, kissing every inch. His rough body pressed against her softness, igniting a pleasure coursing through her veins. Phillips hardness pressed against her stomach, demonstrating his need. Belle slid a hand down between their bodies, wrapping her fingers around him. At the hiss of his breath, Belle smiled her satisfaction at the effect of her touch. She stroked him with long, slow caresses. At each stroke near the top, her thumb rubbed across the wet tip.

Phillip thought he had blacked out from her sensuous touch. Belle undid him. He could handle no more. He must have her now. Phillip rolled Belle over, capturing her hand. He brought it to his lips and slid his tongue along her palm, sliding her thumb into his mouth and softly sucked. Her hips pressed into his, seeking only what he could give her. When she slid her leg over his body, opening herself wide, it was all the encouragement Phillip needed. Without hesitation he slid himself in as slow as possible. Phillip wanted every inch of her surrounding him. Her tightness gripped him, holding on. He stared into her eyes and Belle never blinked, but Phillip noticed her fleeting moment of discomfort. It was then he knew that Belle hadn't been with another man since him. Not even Sheffield. Her eyes shone with devotion. Her gaze formed a memory he would never forget of his time making Belle his again. In every sense of the word. His.

When Phillip slid inside Belle, she felt whole again. Belle opened her heart to have Phillip love her. His eyes revealed the same reflection from the first time they'd made love. His triumph from making Belle his, mind, body, and soul. Only this time they also held a look of sorrow, desperation, and a plea for forgiveness. Belle lifted a hand to his cheek and closed her eyes. When she opened them again, she also saw his fear. Fear that she would refuse. She placed her lips against his, giving him the answer he sought.

When Belle kissed him with everything he wished for, Phillip slid in deeper and paused. Savoring every sensation around them. When her kiss ended, Phillip gave himself to Belle fully. Their bodies became one as they clung tight. He wrapped her in an embrace and tears collected on his chest—tears that scared him. He wanted to comfort Belle, and at the same time Phillip feared she would send him away. So, instead of asking what troubled her, he gathered Belle closer and murmured soothing words of comfort. Belle's tears stopped and she relaxed soft against him, and Phillip realized she'd fallen asleep.

Still, he didn't loosen his hold. Nor did he sleep.

Chapter Eight

Phillip slid out from beneath Belle and slipped on his clothes. The early morning dawn light peeked through the windows. He needed to return home before Henry awakened. Phillip wanted nothing more than to be there when Belle opened her eyes to see if she regretted making love. Phillip had laid awake through the night holding her. He wanted to make love to Belle again. As he pulled on his shoes, Phillip took notice of Belle's bedroom. Decorated with the same fashion as the parlor, one wouldn't expect a madame of a brothel to possess an elegant style. Everything screamed class. Why did Belle follow her life along this path? She could have married well. There were so many questions Phillip wanted to ask, but knew Belle would become defensive if he did. No, he must wait. After their lovemaking, Phillip decided he would never leave her again. Phillip would atone for the rest of his life for the mistakes made by deserting Belle all those years ago.

With one last glance, he left through the door leading to her parlor. Phillip would leave from the room that he entered the evening before. He only hoped there would be no one to witness his departure. Phillip didn't want anyone to think Belle now had a revolving door. He wouldn't tarnish her reputation with falsehoods. The irony didn't go unnoticed by him. Phillip wished to leave a note explaining why he needed to leave, but didn't want the message to fall in unwanted hands. It would be best if he left, then return later to spend more time with Belle.

When he opened the door, it was to find two disgruntled gentlemen waiting. Presumably for him. One would assume Belle was a maiden, and he were sneaking around past her brothers, the way Sheffield and Wildeburg protected her. Phillip shrugged on his coat, nodded, and then moved toward the door. He didn't have to explain himself to these men. What transpired between Belle and him was their own damn business and nobody else's.

"Delamont."

Phillip stopped and rested his head on the door in defeat. The last thing he wanted this morning was to deal with Sheffield. His emotions were a raw, open mess after spending the night with Belle. However, Sheffield wouldn't cower him any longer.

"What do you want and why are you here?" Phillip asked, when he turned around.

"Belle's man, Ned, requested my presence."

"Whatever for?"

"Ned's concern for Belle grew when she dismissed her guard and you never departed. When he entered the parlor and found it empty, and neither one of you exited the room, there was only one place where you could be. Since Belle has never allowed a man in her bedroom—well, except for *one* circumstance," Sheffield glared at Wildeburg, "her behavior was out of the ordinary and raised alarm."

"What do you mean by one circumstance?" He advanced on Wildeburg who sat nonchalantly, wearing a pleased expression. Delamont paid no attention to the rest of Sheffield's explanation. Fury took hold that Wildeburg had shared Belle's charms. Phillip had been certain that nobody had slept with Belle, but him. Usually Wildeburg played the peacemaker, but this time his smile taunted Phillip.

"Yes, that was a very pleasurable afternoon, Sheffield. One I will never forget."

"Nor will I."

"Even after marrying Sophia, you're still perturbed that I bested you?" Wilde laughed.

"Yes, however, I took pleasure in your short demise."

"Which was only short-lived."

"Yes," Sheffield admitted bitterly.

Delamont stood over Wildeburg, ready to punch him. His frustration grew over their conversation which they apparently found amusing. However, Delamont found no humor in their banter. Still Wilde smiled, daring Delamont to punch him.

"Calm down, old man. We are only teasing you." Sheffield slapped Delamont on the back.

"Why would I enjoy hearing how Wildeburg had the pleasure of bedding Rosalyn?"

"My name is Belle. And Wilde never held the pleasure. No man has but you," Belle spoke quietly from behind Delamont.

"But Sheffield implied that Wildeburg shared your bed."

"No, I said that only one man has had the pleasure of visiting Belle's boudoir," stated Sheffield

"And I explained how I enjoyed that afternoon," added Wildeburg.

"Then ..."

"Sheffield, Wilde, stop tormenting him. Wilde shared that afternoon with his wife, Sidney, who at the time was a maiden. He took advantage of the situation and Sheffield exploited it."

"Then you and Wildeburg never ...?"

"No, we never did. I will explain to you later about Wilde's scandalous courtship of Sidney Hartridge at another time. Were you leaving?"

Belle's soft tone sent Phillip to her side at once, the other men forgotten with their sense of torture for a laugh. Her voice held all the insecurity he felt himself. Phillip lifted Belle's chin and placed a soft kiss on her lips. They softened, opening for him. At any other time and without their unwanted company, he would devour her. But he must leave.

"I need to return home before Henry awakens. We have taken to sharing breakfast together, before he begins his studies for the day. With your permission, I would like to return here later."

When Belle had woken and found the bed empty, all her insecurities returned. She thought Phillip had achieved what he wanted and left. At the touch of his warm pillow, she pulled a robe on, hoping to catch him before he left. Belle had opened the door and found Sheffield and Wilde tormenting Phillip. Her doubts fled once she noticed Phillip's anger at their teasing. A few fears remained and always would, but when Phillip explained his reason for leaving so early, she fell even harder for him. He needed to be there for Henry.

"I do not think it would be wise if you returned," Belle said.

"Please, Belle, do not turn me away."

"I allowed you last evening, because I could not endure you not touching me. But I also cannot endure you breaking my heart again. I cannot live through that pain a second time."

Phillip gripped her hand. "I make a solemn promise to you I will not leave again."

"But you will."

"No."

"Yes, it will be inevitable. You must realize that."

"No, I only see you giving me a chance to love you again."

Belle smiled at Phillip as if he were a small child who wouldn't see reason. Phillip wanted to grab her by the shoulders and make Belle understand how he felt.

"Can I return, Belle?"

Belle sighed in defeat. "You may." She only agreed for the opportunity to make him understand why they would never be. It needed a discussion in private without the prying ears in their company.

Phillip didn't care who was present any longer. He pulled Belle into his arms and gave her a kiss filled with enough passion to change her mind. When Belle softened in his arms, Phillip pulled away.

"Until later, my love."

Belle watched Phillip stride from the parlor, closing the door behind him. His confidence strong in every step. She sighed again bringing her fingers to her lips, daydreaming of Phillip. Her friends clearing their throats interrupted her musing. Belle's gaze encountered the amused stares of Sheffield and Wildeburg. Phillip made her forget about them.

A blush seared Belle's cheeks. She gathered her robe tighter. She had never been in a state of undress in front of these men before. Belle felt like an innocent, even though she was anything but.

"Good morning, gentleman."

"Good morning, Belle." Their amusement echoed throughout the room.

"You both know your way out," she spoke over her shoulder, returning to the bedroom.

Belle closed the door and sunk onto the chaise. Her eyes focused on the bed. She would never have peace of mind again. Phillip's presence now filled this sanctuary. His scent invaded her senses. Everywhere Belle looked, she saw Phillip. A simple touch of the bedcovers would remind her of Phillip's caresses. When Belle closed her eyes, she could taste Phillip on her lips.

A thousand regrets overcame her, but one emotion smothered them. Love.

Chapter Nine

When Phillip arrived back at Belle's, Ned met him with a warning, informing Phillip in no uncertain terms how he would enjoy tearing Phillip limb from limb if he so much as made Belle cry. It would seem Belle had enough protectors to last a lifetime. Another person in Belle's life to whom he must prove himself. Phillip showed Ned respect during his lecture and made a vow that he would treat Belle as if she was the most fragile of glass. Phillip's reply didn't appease the brute like he thought it would, if Ned's glare was anything to go by. However, Ned showed Phillip the way to Belle's office.

Phillip stood in the hallway and listened to Belle giving directions to some employees. When confronted with tough questions, he listened with pride when Belle answered each with a fair assessment. The respect her staff paid Belle showed the skilled business woman she had become. When the office emptied, Phillip waited a few minutes before showing himself. If truth be told, nerves held him back.

When he stepped in the doorway, Belle was bent over figures in the ledger book. Concentration drew her teeth over her bottom lip, then she licked it. Phillip groaned at the tempting image. He stepped in and closed the door.

Belle looked up. "My lord, I insist that you please *open* my office door."

Phillip drew Belle from the chair and his lips descended, devouring her with a kiss. He didn't stop with one, stealing one after another. Belle's arms settled around his neck, drawing his head closer. Her fingertips running through the strands of his hair. Phillip needed Belle now. But she broke away from their embrace.

"Lord Delamont," she insisted.

"You called me Phillip last night."

"*Lord Delamont*, I have an image to uphold. If any of my customers were to get wind of the liberties I allowed you, they would assume they could enjoy the same. Over the years I have built a reputation as being unattainable and I will not allow you to ruin that for me."

"Hell would have to freeze over before I ever allowed another gentleman to take his pleasure with you. Even then it would never be possible."

"In my line of work, that is not always an option. Now please open the door or I will have Ned show you the way out." Belle sat back down at the desk, shuffling paperwork.

If Phillip wanted any chance with Belle this afternoon, they he must abide by her wishes. He wanted to demand that she no longer had to concern herself with business. But Phillip saw Belle's stubbornness and pride in her empire. She wouldn't let the place go easily. No, it would be best to approach his position in Belle's life in another direction. To force Belle into his wishes would only end in bitterness. He needed to rebuild their relationship before demanding anything. Phillip knew what he wanted. While it was highly improper and would close many doors, he didn't care. Phillip would find a way for them to be together forever. A family. Something he had wanted since the first day he met Belle.

"Sorry, love. Your beauty prompted an overwhelming need to kiss your sweet lips. I have waited all morning to savor them under my own."

Phillip opened the door and sat in a chair. He would flood her with compliments, shock Belle with improper thoughts, and consume her with kisses. In the end he would strip away every one of Belle's defenses.

"Do not think for one second that I have fallen for your charm, Lord Delamont."

"You haven't? Well then, I must try harder."

"You can try, but over the years many scandalous rakes have tried and I am nothing but immune to empty words."

"Ahh, but mine are not empty. They're full of promises of pleasures to come."

"What pleasures might those be?" Belle enjoyed the light flirtation.

Phillip looked over his shoulder to see if anyone lingered in the hallway. He then leaned over the desk, urging her to come closer.

"The kind where my kisses caress every silkiness inch of your skin until you cry my name aloud, begging for me to never stop," Phillip whispered.

"And would you?"

"Would I what?"

"Stop."

"Yes." Phillip relaxed back in the chair.

"Yes?"

"Yes, but only because my kisses would be replaced by my cock sliding into your hot wetness, slowly. So slow that your body will hum with satisfaction from every sensation when I'm inside you. Where you will clench me tight and throb your pleasure around me. Then I would take you and make you mine over and over with every stroke. And throughout our passion, you will cling to me begging the same as before."

"For you to never stop?"

"Yes."

"Yes," Belle moaned, now regretting to ask him to open the door.

With every whispered word, the man seduced Belle into a wanton woman. Her breasts grew heavy, nipples were tightening under the gown. The ache between her thighs grew wet and throbbed with his promises. Belle wanted Phillip now. She wanted to lay bare before him while he worshipped her with his mouth. She longed to have his body press into hers and take her with long, slow strokes. Belle needed Phillip's touch. The taste of his lips.

Belle cleared her throat, rising from the desk.

"Perhaps this conversation is best to have in my parlor. We should be more comfortable there."

Belle didn't wait for Phillip to answer and continued to the private parlor, certain he would follow. The wicked desire in Phillip's eyes had been present since he arrived.

Phillip locked the door. Nobody would disturb their time together now or later. He wanted Belle to himself for the afternoon and all evening if he could. Phillip pressed Belle against the door, pulling her skirts higher. Her fingers fumbled to unfasten his trousers. Their need clear. When she wrapped a hand around his cock, he slid his fingers inside her core, sinking into her wetness. Belle's desire was as powerful as Phillip's. She guided him to lift her leg over his hip.

With one swift stroke, Phillip entered Belle. All of his whispered words would have to wait for later. He needed to be inside of her now. Belle dropped her head back against the door as Phillip took possession of her body. Her moans echoing around them. She clung to his shoulders as he rode her sweet body.

Belle pushed her hips into Phillip, urging him to take her faster. His body possessed her soul, and she opened herself to him. She needed more. Belle was greedy for the satisfaction only Phillip could give. His strokes grew more frantic, fast, and hard with a need that only seemed to grow. Still, it didn't ease the ache.

"Please do not ever stop," Belle whispered, begging him like he said she would.

The words Phillip wished to hear, Belle cried with pleasure. Phillip exploded inside her, taking them flying to the sweetest abyss.

Phillip lifted Belle and carried her to the bedroom, locking that door too. He still had many more ways to love her. He stripped them of their clothes, caressing her skin with his lips like he promised. Phillip spent the rest of the afternoon loving her with those promises and making more as he went along. Not one part of her body did he neglect. It wasn't long before she begged for him to never stop and he obliged her with more pleasure. He would never be able to get enough of her after his years of starvation.

After endless hours, Belle lay in Phillip's embrace, her body sated time and time again. Yet, she still ached to have him take her again. Belle's fingers trailed across Phillip's chest. She placed a soft kiss here and there.

"The hour grows late. Do you need to return home to Henry?"

"No, I am yours for the evening." He rolled over, rising above her.

"I must return to work. Will you stay till I am finished? We never had our discussion."

Phillip kissed her forehead. "I will wait for you for an eternity, if only for a second of your time."

"Oh, he lays on the charm again. There is no need, my lord. You have already had the pleasure of my body. No need to become poetic with me."

"Ah, Belle, one day you will learn that what I speak is only the truth from my heart."

Belle lowered her lashes, not wanting him to see the reflection in her eyes of how that made her feel. Phillip's words touched too close to her heart. Belle wasn't ready for him to know how he affected her. Even though she offered him her body, she still didn't trust him.

Phillip rolled over and helped Belle from the bed. He relaxed against the pillows and watched her dress for the evening. The transformation astounded him. The simple day dress Belle wore in her office paled compared to the revealing gown she changed into. Phillip tampered down his jealousy. He knew every gentleman Belle encountered would attempt to seduce her. However, Phillip trusted Belle. She wouldn't stray. If no man had ever tempted Belle in all these years, then none would now.

While Belle styled her hair, Phillip got dressed. When she stood in front of the mirror, he stood behind and kissed her shoulder. Phillip trailed his lips along her neck.

"I want to make love to you in front of this mirror. I want you to watch the passion in your eyes when I make you mine," Phillip whispered.

Belle's gaze met Phillip's in the mirror. The image staring back now wasn't the same woman she had created over the years. No, this was a woman who wanted to be owned by this man. And she wanted to own him.

Mind, body, and soul.

Chapter Ten

Over the next several weeks they settled into a routine. Phillip would spend his evenings making love to Belle and return home to Henry in the morning. Throughout the day they each would go about their own business. Occasionally, they would meet at the park. An innocent meeting between Lord Delamont and Rosie. The bond between Rosie and Henry strengthened in its own right. Phillip enjoyed watching the mischief between the two.

They hadn't spoken of his reasons for leaving Belle all those years ago. Every time Phillip tried to discuss the subject, Belle tempted him into forgetting his thoughts, capturing Phillip under her spell.

Even her friends had stepped back to let their relationship find its own path. The women were more than encouraging, even offering Phillip advice on how to woo Belle. Not that he needed any. Belle seemed to enjoy his pursuit as long as he kept it lighthearted. Whenever he became serious and broached their future, she would put space between them. Phillip hoped in time Belle would relent, but for now there was a wall of defense he had yet to climb over.

On the other hand, Sheffield and company may not have been so encouraging, but they allowed him to pursue Belle without interfering. Sheffield and Beckwith even invited Phillip along to Lord Hartridge's home for lively discussions. He was most surprised to see Lady Sidney amongst the men, arguing her viewpoint. Sheffield and Sidney usually ended the discussions in a heated argument. While both of their points held merit,

Lady Sidney didn't back down from disagreeing with Sheffield. Soon, Wildeburg and Sophia would sweep in and separate the two. The conversation would change, and Sidney and Sheffield would be laughing again. Phillip noticed the respect Sheffield held for Sidney. A trait he would never have imagined Sheffield to hold for any woman. It would seem the arrogance of his old friend had softened.

Phillip mentioned this to Belle one evening while sharing dinner. She laughed and explained the dynamics of her friends' marriages and how they came to be, including her involvement.

"So that is the meaning behind what Kathleen spoke when she mentioned that they owed all their marriages to you."

Belle's eyes lit at the sincerity of Kathleen's compliment. "How sweet of her to say so."

"You do not realize how special you are to them, do you?"

"You speak nonsense."

"No, I do not. They have been very protective of our courtship."

"Yes, well ..." There were no words Belle could answer Phillip with. To do so, would open herself to him.

Belle was determined to have their relationship stay carefree with neither one of them making genuine promises they couldn't keep. Endearments whispered in passion and pillow-talk weren't considered any commitments. Belle would allow whatever this was to run its course. After their affair ended, she wanted to find a cottage in the country to live her remaining days. She'd grown tired of the double life she led. After spending these last few weeks with Phillip, Belle realized that she fooled herself into believing that she found contentment in life being a successful business woman.

Belle had tried to create an impossible dream and now that she faced the reality of it, she wished to find peace. Belle wanted to be *herself* again. Not Rosie, the widow who tried to be common and fit in with the lower gentry. Not Belle, the esteemed Madame that nobody would dare cross—the woman that every gentleman in the ton wished to bed, and every woman wished to be. No, she wanted to be Rosalyn again.

But not the Rosalyn who was naïve enough to believe that somebody of Phillip's stature would ever marry her, and they would live happily ever after. No, she wanted to be the woman who, at one time, had the fortune to be loved by a man that she loved in return. Someone who would cherish those memories while living a simple life. A life without the drama, suspense, and the fear of someone exposing Belle as a fraud. For now, Belle would enjoy these moments with Phillip and store the memories for a time to come. Later, when Belle was left all alone, she would reflect on them. Without Phillip.

Ned knocked on the door, saving Belle from further questions from Phillip. They spoke quietly, and she gave Ned instructions. She returned to Phillip's side, brushing her lips across his cheek.

"I am afraid I must cut our dinner short. I am needed on the floor. Can you see yourself out?"

"I will wait."

Belle needed Phillip to leave. There was a crisis she must attend to. Phillip would only be a distraction and would cause greater problems. His presence on a nightly basis already caused rumors to spread. Belle had hoped to keep their relationship private, but Phillip made no secret of his affections for her, and speculation arose.

Belle started to dissuade Phillip from staying, but Ned returned with a demand for her immediate attention. She swept out the door behind Ned.

Belle assumed Phillip would stay and await her return, reading as he usually did. But instead he followed.

When Belle entered the card room, it was to find Lord Velden sitting at a table flanked by two of his guards. Velden had pushed his way inside and refused to leave. Belle had revoked Velden's membership a few months ago after a card game against Kathleen and Holdenburg. With the help of Beckwith, Sheffield, Wildeburg, and many influential gentlemen of the ton, they ran Velden out of London. It would appear that he didn't heed their threat. And to add to her troubles, Velden had employed Brutus and Magnus for his guards. They used to fight for Belle at The Scuffle. But after beating Beckwith senseless while he was drunk and unaware of his faculties, Belle denied them another fight and spread word around London of their aggressive behavior. All the fighting venues refused to allow them to compete. With their presence here, Belle suddenly felt the threat of enemies who could ruin her. Oh, she'd angered many men over the years, but never crossed the line so as to have anybody want to destroy her.

From the look in Lord Velden's eyes, he had only one goal, and that was to see to Belle's demise. Even though Velden brought on his exile with his own actions, he laid the blame at Belle's feet because she allowed it to happen here.

"Lord Velden, your membership in no longer valid."

"Yes, I am well aware of that. I only stopped by to let you know that I have proposed a bill in Parliament to shut down places like your establishment. Houses of ill-repute are demeaning to our society and only bring conflict to esteemed families."

"What has made you take the higher moral ground? You have enjoyed the pleasures of my *establishment* for years."

"After my ordeal, I saw the error of my ways in the immoral sins I committed. I have many supporters for the bill. I have gained their support by using the Prince Regent as an example and they grow weary of the shame he creates for the monarchy with his indecent scandals. With their support, many others will fall behind my agenda."

"Very clever of you, Lord Velden. I thank you for the warning. Now, if you will please take your leave before I enforce your exit."

With that, Belle turned and left. She wouldn't give Lord Velden the benefit of arguing the unfairness of his declaration. That was what he wanted. Nor would Belle show any fear in front of customers and staff. If Velden had organized the support he claimed, then he could destroy Belle. Not even with the power Sheffield yielded would he be able to save her. Belle's establishment would be the first to close, because Prinny himself was a regular visitor. A charming man, but a menace all the same. His gluttony well known amongst her girls.

Belle headed for the office to write a message for Sheffield. She would need his guidance on how to proceed. Belle also needed to warn Devon and Kathleen that Lord Velden had never left town. Kathleen's life could be in danger. Since Lord Velden threatened Belle, he might seek vengeance against Kathleen too. Through Kathleen's revenge, Velden had been shamed and ousted.

"Ned, please deliver these notes to Sheffield and Holdenburg."

Phillip had observed the exchange between Belle and Lord Velden. He admired Belle's courage when she coolly dismissed Velden's threat—a threat that would work to his advantage, if he aligned himself with Lord Velden. However, Phillip knew of the underhanded techniques of Velden and wouldn't support him. Also, he wouldn't scheme to convince Belle of the alternative life they could share. No, Phillip would win her hand fair and square. If only Belle would let him. Phillip didn't know whether to be furious or disappointed that Belle still turned to Sheffield with her troubles. Phillip held as much influence, if not more, than Sheffield.

"Why are you sending for Sheffield?"

"Because he would know how best to advise me on this situation."

"Why do you not seek my advice?"

Belle sighed. She heard the disappointment in Phillip's voice, but she wouldn't soothe his wounded ego. Belle would never ask Phillip for help with her business. She knew Phillip didn't approve and only kept quiet out of fear of losing their time together. With this latest development, perhaps it would be best to end their relationship now? Lord Velden wouldn't go away without a fight, and she didn't wish to drag Phillip through a scandal. It wouldn't be fair to him or Henry.

"I have always sought Sheffield's advice when troubles arise. His influence settles any conflicts."

"You no longer need Sheffield. I hold as much power as he does."

"Yes, you do."

"Still, you choose him."

"It is not a matter of choice."

"How not?"

She said pointedly, "Phillip, I trust him."

Belle's words knocked Phillip down. Apparently, it seemed their time together was only ever an illusion. While Phillip patiently waited for Belle to overcome their past, she had only been toying with his emotions. Belle never planned for this to go any further than what they shared in bed. When Phillip stared into Belle's eyes, he finally saw what he had fooled himself into believing. There would be nothing for him to say otherwise. No amount of pleading for forgiveness would change that she would never again *trust* him.

"And you will never hold that trust in me." Phillip didn't ask her a question, he only stated what was now obvious.

Belle chose not to answer. There was no way to respond without lying. Belle didn't think she would ever trust Phillip again. Her heart hadn't forgiven him for his ultimate betrayal from the past.

Belle's silence expressed it all.

Phillip had nothing more to say, for now. He needed time to think on his next course of action. Phillip wouldn't give up on them. But he hurt too much to stay and witness her knight in shining armor, Sheffield, come to the rescue again. Phillip decided to leave. But he would return, there would be no mistake on that.

Phillip walked out of Belle's office without a word of farewell. Belle knew she had cut him deeply, but didn't expect him to leave like that. Belle touched her breast, the pain seeping in.

It would seem her heart wasn't so well-guarded after all.

Chapter Eleven

Belle arrived at the park early, not wanting to miss a chance at catching a glimpse of Phillip. She missed lying in his arms through the night. It had been a week since he'd walked out. Belle hadn't heard a word from him. She tried not to feel rejected. The fault lay with Belle after deeply hurting him.

He no longer brought Henry to the park. However, Henry came every day to play with his friends. His trusting smile while he ate his biscuit gave Belle reassurance that Phillip wouldn't cut her from the boy's life. Henry's new governess would accompany him and sit on a bench nearby, always keeping a watchful eye on her charge. She was a young girl with a warm disposition. Henry introduced Belle to Lucy, explaining that Rosie was his friend. Lucy replied that Lord Delamont had spoken of their friendship, and that she was to allow Henry all the time he wanted with Rosie. It warmed Belle's heart that Phillip considered her advice on the kind of governess Henry needed. Belle wanted to ask Henry why his father no longer joined him, but pride kept her silent.

One day, when Henry waved goodbye, Belle decided to leave too. She trailed behind them at a discreet pace. When Belle came to the park entrance, she wished to continue following them but stopped, knowing she would look out of place in Henry's neighborhood. Before, it had been out of anger for the lad's welfare. Today's reason would be for selfish purposes.

When Belle was about to turn toward home, street thugs set upon Henry and Lucy. Belle watched in horror when they stole the governess's reticule and shoved her to the ground. When Henry tried to defend Lucy, they struck him across the face sending him flying backwards. Henry landed in a heap, his arm twisted at an odd angle. Belle shouted for help and ran toward them. When she got closer, she saw they were not street thugs, but Brutus and Magnus. This was not a random attack, but one done out of vengeance. Did her association with Phillip put Henry in danger? At her pounding footsteps coming towards them, the brutes took off. A crowd gathered, coming to their aid. Belle ran to Henry and brushed the hair from his face. He moaned. Tears ran down Belle's cheek at the vicious attack. A bruise was appearing under Henry's eye.

"Rosie?"

"Yes love, 'tis I. How do you feel, dear?"

"Did you see me defend Lucy?"

"Yes, dear. You are a brave knight in shining armor. Can you walk?"

Henry groaned in agony when he tried to push himself up with his arm. Belle caught him before he fell.

"My arm hurts badly."

Belle looked around for help. The crowd had helped Lucy to her feet and someone was giving an account of the attack to a constable.

"Wait here, love. I will get you home."

Belle hired a hackney. The driver, who saw the attack, told Belle he had a child of his own and insisted on helping. After they were settled, Henry cried for Belle to come home with him. He was scared and wanted her comfort. Belle couldn't deny him and wanted to ease Lucy's anxiety. Lucy feared for her job, after hearing how the other servants were dismissed because they neglected Henry's welfare. Belle tried to reassure Lucy that it wasn't her fault and Lord Delamont wouldn't dismiss her. If any blame were to be laid, it would be toward Belle. Belle had brought danger into their lives with her nefarious lifestyle.

The hackney driver lifted Henry in his arms and followed Belle and Lucy to the front door. Belle didn't wait but opened the door to a startled footman and butler. She gave them directions and after their initial shock they immediately followed her demands. The housekeeper bustled Lucy to the kitchen to see to her injuries and to calm the nanny's nerves with a pot of tea. The footman took Henry from the hackney driver and carried him to his room. Another footman left to gather a doctor at the butler's direction. Belle thanked the hackney driver and followed the commotion to Henry's room. She saw to his comfort, helping Henry off with his coat and holding him while he wept. Her gentle soothing calmed him enough to endure his pain.

The butler brought the doctor in and Belle stood nearby. The doctor explained that Henry only suffered from a slight sprain and would need to wear his arm in a sling for a few days. He left a bottle of laudanum for Henry's pain and to help him sleep. Belle slipped the bottle into a pocket. She wouldn't allow a soul to give Henry this medicine. She had watched too many people become addicted. Instead, she would give instructions on a special poultice to help soothe the boy's injuries.

The butler, called Miles, informed Belle that Lord Delamont was away in meetings for the day and he didn't know when he would return. Miles treated Belle with the respect one would a lady.

Soon the housekeeper arrived with a pot of tea and sandwiches. She fussed over Henry and promised to have cook bake his special biscuits. When all the servants came and went throughout the afternoon to see to Henry's comfort, they each showed their respect toward Belle. Which caused Belle to grow more confused. When the cook herself delivered the biscuits, the housekeeper pulled Belle to the side, inquiring if there were anything she needed. Belle questioned her as to why the warm welcome. The housekeeper only patted her hand and said it was because the master deemed it to be so. The servants were all given instructions to welcome Belle in Lord Delamont's home with the same kindness and warmth they showed him and Henry.

It shocked Belle that Phillip would speak of her to anybody, let alone his servants. She went back into Henry's room and read him a story. After he drifted to sleep, she pondered these new circumstances the rest of the afternoon.

Belle needed to send word to Sheffield about the threat. However, she owed Phillip an explanation first—the incident involved his son. Belle tried to process his staff's treatment. Had she been wrong not to trust in Phillip? Was it fair to hold Phillip's past mistakes over his head? He'd displayed time and time again the depth of his feelings for her. Belle's despicable treatment in his home at the hands of the previous butler had prompted Phillip to speak with his servants on how to treat Belle if she were to return. That alone showed how much he cared.

Henry whimpered in his sleep. Belle took off her shoes and crawled on the bed. She brought Henry into her arms and whispered words of comfort until he quieted down. Belle continued to hold him as if she were his mother. After many sleepless nights, Belle succumbed to the warmth of the room and slipped away in slumber.

~~~~

When Phillip entered Henry's room, this was how he found them. They appeared as a mother wrapping her son in a protective barrier. His heart softened at the sight. Then it quickly hardened again. If it weren't for Belle,

Henry would never have been harmed. He had stayed away on purpose this past week. If she wouldn't trust him, then Phillip would prove to Belle she could. Phillip had taken steps to end Lord Velden's revenge. It would seem he did hold just as much power as Sheffield with Parliament. The lords of the realm listened to his opinions and agreed that if they shut down establishments like Belle's, it would only cause unscrupulous people to open underground clubs allowing activities more deprived. He explained how Belle kept a clean brothel, insisting on monthly medical exams for her girls, and the gambling club only allowed members of the ton who could afford to gamble. If at any time anyone didn't abide by her rules, she would revoke their membership.

They were most impressed and decided to withdraw Lord Velden's request. They also realized that the only way to curb the Prince Regent's scandalous activities were to hire men to cover the Prince's tracks better.

Lord Velden must have gotten word of his involvement and thought to send him a message. Well, Phillip read it loud and clear. Anyone who went after his family would receive their own message in return. Before he sought his revenge, he would need to make sure Henry was well and send him away until this mess cleared.

Phillip had neglected his priorities. Instead of seeing to Henry's welfare, he'd allowed a woman's affections to rule his actions. Henry was the only one left in Phillip's life. He thought the woman laying with his son would be too. However, Belle made her feelings clear. He'd been too blind to see them. Phillip knew removing Belle from Henry's life would be hard for the boy, but his safety was more important.

Phillip touched Belle's shoulder, shaking her awake. Her eyelids fluttered open. She stared at him in confusion and then glanced around the room. When Belle remembered why she was here and opened her mouth,

Phillip placed his finger to her lips. Belle nodded, and he helped her from the bed. Holding Belle's hand, Phillip led the way down the hall to his bedroom.

Belle's hand rested in Phillip's grasp. For the first time in a week, she felt his touch. Her heart lightened once again, believing that all would be well between them. When Phillip arrived at the bedroom, the familiar pull of attraction that her body ached to ease overtook her senses. However, once Phillip closed the door, he dropped her hand and walked away to stare out the windows. Belle stood rooted near the door, sensing his change of mood wasn't for the better.

Phillip stared outside, gathering his emotions under control. He should have never touched her. It conflicted with his emotions. One minute he wanted to spout his fury, the next he wanted to pull her in his arms and spend the rest of evening making love. But then all he had to do was to remember his son lying in pain. Pain, that if not for her, Henry would never have had to suffer.

"Madame, perhaps you can explain the incident involving my son's injuries from this afternoon?"

Belle shivered at the chill in Phillip's voice. If there were a distance between them before, it certainly divided them now. Not only was his voice cold, but the look of disgust in his eyes was something Belle knew would happen one day. Yes, she had held out hope that she would never witness that stare, but in reality knew she always would. Their affair, while precious, was only a passing of time. Never meant to last long. Belle stiffened and straightened her shoulders. And prepared for the worst.

"Your son and governess were set upon by thugs. It appeared to be a robbery, but when I ran to their defense, I noticed their assailants. They were two men by the name of Brutus and Magnus, the two guards who accompanied Lord Velden to my club earlier in the week."

"So because of you, Henry lies in pain. Because of your *lifestyle*, harm was brought upon the only person I love."

Phillip's insult slammed in Belle's gut. He made it clear he held no love for her, only for Henry. Belle stood still, not blinking. She wouldn't give Phillip the satisfaction of knowing that his words cut her soul into shreds. Belle wouldn't weep for this man.

"It would appear so. I do not understand why they would target him, or you, for that matter."

"Do you not? Perhaps could it be that I have shared your bed nightly over the course of the last few weeks? Do you think our affair has gone unnoticed to the members of your club? We are on the tongues of every peer of the ton."

"But we have been discreet."

"Madame, you know as well as I do that word does not exist in the world we live in."

"Still, I do not understand why they would attack Henry."

"Then let me explain it to you in simple terms."

Phillip's condescending tone grated on her nerves. He spoke as if she were a simpleton, not worthy of his respect. Belle's hands tightened into fists. She would listen to his explanation. Then she would leave, but not before she gave an opinion of her own.

"Because of my infatuation with you and your lack of trust in my ability to help you with your problems, I took it upon myself to fix them. I have stopped Lord Velden's plans to close your establishment."

As Phillip explained his reasons, he advanced toward Belle, standing but a breath away. He leaned closer. "If I had not been so obsessed with the very need of you. The need to possess you and make you mine. To share every waking moment near you. To think I wanted to spend the rest of my life with you. If this overpowering desire had not consumed me, I would never have fought for you. All to earn a trust you had no intention of giving me. Even now I want you. I want to throw you on my bed and take whatever you will give me."

Before Belle could object Phillip took possession of her mouth with every ounce of anger he held. He controlled the kiss, taking from her soul. Phillip meant to punish Belle, but he was a drowning man once their lips touched. Each pull of her lips he demanded, and she responded with her own demands. When Belle softened and her body swayed for his arms to take hold, Phillip pulled away in disgust.

"You are not the girl I fell in love with all those years ago. You are a creature who repulses me with your sinful temptations."

Phillip regretted his hateful words the second they left his mouth. His anger was at himself for giving into his desires, but he took it out on Belle. He never meant them. Instantly, he tried reaching out to Belle to apologize when her face paled and the anguish piercing her eyes shamed him.

Belle jerked backward as if Phillip had slapped her. She never imagined he held such hatred. Belle was a fool for giving into his kiss. Her next words were spoken softly, but yet they echoed around the room.

"Your callous disregard killed that young miss all those years ago, and you only have yourself to blame for the creature I became. You have made yourself clear that you hold no affection for me. I was a fool and gave myself to you against my better judgement. I will make no such mistake again. Furthermore, I did not ask for your assistance. For your need to interfere, the fault only lies with you. My heart aches for Henry's suffering and I will regret it until I die. I have never set out to harm any child *of yours*. I only ever wanted to love you."

Belle turned and left. She walked out of Phillip's home with as much dignity that she could muster. Her soul crumbled inside, but Belle didn't look back once. She kept moving, one step at a time, drawing herself farther and farther away from Phillip.

Chapter Twelve

Phillip rested in a chair in the darkened bedroom, watching over Henry sleeping. The memory of Belle's pain rested in this gut. The anguish in her voice would forever surround him. There was no amount of justification to his comments. Phillip blamed Belle for his own actions. What made it even worse, Henry kept asking for Belle throughout the night. It was Belle's comfort he sought, not his father's. How would he ever be able to repair the damage?

Phillip fell asleep wondering if Belle would forgive him. He was woken a few hours later by the sun streaming through the windows. Phillip wiped the sleep from his eyes and watched Henry come awake.

"Rosie?"

"She has returned home, son."

Henry's crestfallen face said it all. He missed Belle as much as Phillip did.

"But she will return, won't she?"

"It is highly unlikely."

"Why not?"

"Your father is a fool, my boy. I am afraid I hurt Rosie's feelings."

"Just tell her you are sorry. Rosie will forgive you. She has a big heart, Papa."

Such innocent words, and so true. Belle did, but after Phillip's rant, her heart would no longer be open to him again.

"Perhaps, once you have mended, I can offer my apologies when I take you to visit the park."

"No, Papa you have to try today. I wish for her to visit me. She promised to bring me my favorite biscuits for being so brave yesterday. She called me a knight."

"Is that so? Why did she refer to you as a knight?"

Henry regaled Phillip with his version of saving Lucy when the men stole her reticule. How he kicked and hit them with his fists. Then he explained how Rosie caused a commotion to scare them away. He also told Phillip that Rosie saw to his and Lucy's care, hiring a hackney and seeing them home.

"Then she ordered the servants around, telling them how to nurse Lucy and me. She cared for us, like how mama used to. It felt nice, Papa."

Phillip was an even bigger fool than he first thought. Instead of blaming her, he should have been singing her praises. With her swift thinking, Belle saved them from suffering further harm. With concern for their welfare, Belle put Henry and Lucy first above all others.

Phillip promised Henry he would find Rosie and apologize. After luncheon, Phillip told Henry once he returned they would spend the afternoon playing games. Phillip asked Miles to have Lucy sit with Henry until his return. Before he left, he questioned Lucy on yesterday's event. Her nervous replies confirmed Henry's story. Throughout the morning, all his servants sang Belle's praises. Only causing Phillip more shame.

~~~~~

Belle only returned home long enough to pack a valise. She couldn't stay where so many memories were so recently created. Phillip's presence was in every room, on every piece of furniture. Everywhere she looked. Belle informed Ned of her whereabouts and swore him to secrecy. Then Belle went to the only place where she could seek the comfort she needed.

She knocked on Sheffield's door, hoping she hadn't made a mistake by coming to his home. Even though Sophia and Alex often invited her here, Belle always refused. She didn't want to bring shame onto them. When Mason showed her in, Belle heard laughter coming down the hallway and Belle realized she had called at an inappropriate time. She tried backing out the doorway, but the butler insisted that she follow him. Mason showed her into an elegantly decorated parlor, Sophia's touch evident everywhere she looked. Belle waited for Sheffield to arrive, her eyes darting at every sound. She would flee at a moment's notice if anybody other than Alex or Sophia entered.

Sophia opened the door to find her dear friend in misery. With one look she saw the heartache pouring from Belle's eyes. Sophia held her arms wide and Belle ran into them. She clung to Sophia and cried out her heartache. Sophia guided them to the sofa, allowing Belle her grief. Sophia thought Lord Delamont had redeemed himself, but if Belle's tears were any sign, he had only broken her heart again. Alex would be furious when he discovered Belle crying in their parlor.

"What has he done?"

"I am so ashamed. You have guests, I should not have come here. I will only bring shame to you as I have done to him."

"What nonsense you speak. Belle, you are part of our family. What did Lord Delamont say to you?"

"Phillip called me a sinful creature who has brought trouble to his family."

Sophia bit back every angry comment she wanted to make toward Lord Delamont. How dare he slander her friend? And to think Sophia vouched for him.

"What nonsense."

"He also admitted that the only person he loved was his son. Phillip does not even love me, Phee. What a fool I have been."

"You are not the fool, Belle. Delamont is."

Belle burst into tears again. Sophia's faithfulness undid Belle. Between fits of crying she told Sophia what happened to Henry. Then Belle told Sophia of the horrible row she had with Phillip. Sophia assured Belle that none of this was her fault.

Sophia insisted that Belle spend a few days with them until she could make a decision. She asked Mason to inform the staff to prepare a room. Sophia guided Belle into a room decorated in soft shades of lavender. The place soothed Belle immediately. Sophia dismissed the maid and helped Belle prepare for bed. She even held her hand when Belle continued with her tears in bed. When Alex appeared in the doorway, Sophia shook her head not to disturb them. He nodded and left. Once Belle drifted to sleep, Sophia went to their bedroom where she found Alex pacing back and forth.

"What happened?" Alex demanded.

Sophia explained, and her husband's mood changed from being worried about Belle to fury at Lord Delamont. Sophia needed to calm Alex before he did anything rash.

He said, "I was curious on who convinced Lord Velden's supporters to stop the bill. I planned to visit Belle tomorrow to give her the excellent news. Why would Delamont go to the trouble of helping Belle only to destroy her with his disgust?"

"I do not know, Alex. I fear it was because of the attack on his son."

"His fear is understandable. But from all accounts, Belle saved the lad from the attackers."

"Fear can prompt many to say things they do not mean," Sophia gently reminded him.

"I will not allow him any measure on this, Phee. You cannot compare their story to ours."

"Can I not? He is but a man that does not understand his emotions and acted out of fear."

"He is nothing but a fool. I allowed you to persuade me into letting their relationship run its course. But no longer. I will protect Belle from Delamont. She will stay with us until she is ready to move on with her life."

"I already told her this."

Alex drew Sophia into his arms. "Thank you for understanding my friendship with Belle, and opening your arms to her." Alex placed a soft kiss upon her lips.

"There is no need to thank me, sweet husband. Belle is as much my friend as yours." Sophia returned his kiss with a soft one of her own.

"Because of her, we would never have been. With your help, I vow to help Belle find happiness." Alex would do anything for Belle.

~~~~~

Phillip pounded on the door. He'd waited outside for over an hour and nobody would let him inside. Since his arrival, there had been no activity. Not one carriage brought any customers to the door. Nobody came or left. But he heard voices coming through the window. He leaned his back against the door. Phillip had received Belle's message loud and clear. Belle didn't wish to see him and he couldn't blame her. Phillip had acted like an ass. Yesterday, he promised Henry that he would make right by Rosie, but he had been too much of a coward. He couldn't face his own shame, so he lied to Henry, telling him that Rosie wished to be alone for a few days. Phillip vowed he would try again tomorrow. Well tomorrow had arrived and Phillip had gotten no further on his apology.

He had lied to Henry yesterday, but Belle didn't. She may not have visited, but Belle sent Henry a package with a note. Henry read the note, laughing, and opened the gift. They were just as she promised; a tin full of his favorite biscuits. When Phillip inquired to what the note said, Henry handed it to him.

Sir Henry,

If ever there were a knight more deserving of these lemon drop biscuits, I know of no other braver than you. My promise to visit you this afternoon, I must break. I have no excuse other than to say I feel awful for your accident. I am most sincerely sorry.

Now then, I expect you to eat all these delicious treats and on the morrow you shall receive more. And each day until your arm is mended. By then your papa will probably have to roll you out bed. I can imagine the sight now.

Take care, my love. I hope to visit you soon.

Your devoted friend,

Rosie

Phillip ran his hand through his hair in frustration, walking back and forth on the sidewalk in front of Belle's home. How had Phillip not seen that Belle loved his son as if he were her own? And Henry loved her too. All the signs were there; Belle ruffling Henry's hair, her gentle smile when she listened to his stories, and Henry slipping his hand in Belle's when walking in the park. Henry should have been their child together. If he hadn't married Julia all those years ago, Belle and he would have their own child to love, nay children. He walked around to the back garden and sat on a bench. Phillip would wait all day and night for a chance to apologize.

~~~~~

Ned followed the bloke around the house. When he watched Lord Delamont sit on a bench, he realized the man wouldn't be leaving anytime soon. He slipped back inside, watching him from behind the drapes. When Sheffield looked over Ned's shoulder, he shook his head in disgust.

"He ain't leaving," said Ned.

"No, I do not suppose he will."

"Do you want me to inform him Belle is not here?"

"Not right now. Let him suffer a while longer. He might as well, because Belle sure as hell is."

Ned shook his head at Sheffield's coldness. While the bastard deserved to suffer for his treatment of Belle, he also knew Belle wouldn't wish it so. His mistress's kindness for the underdog was what made him pledge his devotion. Belle always wished happiness for others, and it was time she received some for herself. With one last glance at Delamont, he continued to help Sheffield. Belle had made a few requests and Ned wanted to make sure he followed through with them.

It was much later after Sheffield's departure that Ned remembered Delamont. When he looked out the window he noticed the man huddled in his coat, rubbing his hands together to keep warm. Ned decided to take pity on the poor bastard. He grabbed a bottle of Belle's finest whiskey and sat down on the same bench. Ned took a long drink and handed the bottle to Delamont. Delamont looked at him with suspicion and Ned nodded to the bottle.

Delamont grabbed the whiskey, keeping one eye on Ned when he drank from the bottle with a thirst unknown to him. The fiery liquid burned his throat and started a roaring fire in his gut. As his insides warmed, he drank more hoping that the fire would seep to his outside. As the day had worn on with still no sign of Belle, a sense of despair had overcome him.

"Belle is not here. She hasn't been since yesterday." Ned told him.

"Then why not open the door and tell me she was not at home?" Delamont kept drinking.

"Sheffield wanted you to suffer."

Delamont laughed, the sound turning bitter. Sheffield. He should have known. Delamont didn't even need to ask Ned if that was where Belle hid herself. He already knew. Well, it looked like he needed to move his vigil to Sheffield's home. He'd made a promise to Henry he needed to keep—and a promise to himself.

Delamont stood. "Do you mind?" he asked Ned, indicating the bottle.

"It is all yours."

Delamont nodded and walked into the darkness.

"There is no more use for it here anymore," Ned said to the empty garden with a grin on his face.

Chapter Thirteen

The loud pounding didn't go unnoticed by Sophia as she hurried to the foyer. When Mason opened the door, a drunken Lord Delamont sauntered in. She folded her arms and tapped her foot in annoyance at his rude behavior.

"Ah, Your Grace, how lovely to see you," slurred Delamont.

Sophia rolled her eyes. She ordered Mason to bring a strong brew of coffee to the parlor. She then turned and strolled down to the darkest corner of the hallway. Sophia looked over her shoulder and when Phillip didn't follow she arched her eyebrow the exact same way Sheffield did. An annoying trait on Sheffield, on the duchess it demanded respect. He followed Sophia into a small parlor. Phillip realized where she had led him. To the same type of parlor his butler placed Belle in his own home all those weeks ago.

The place for unwelcome guests.

Phillip slumped in the chair, bringing the bottle to his lips for another drop of courage. Sophia humphed and held out her hand, and he sighed, handing the bottle over. When the butler brought in the tray, Sophia passed the spirits over to Mason with disgust. She sat down elegantly, pouring Phillip a cup of coffee. She pushed it near him and sat back as regal as a queen.

"Drink," Sophia ordered.

She continued to glare at Phillip while he sipped at the warm brew. In their short time together, he had never known Sophia to be anything but a warm and generous woman. Her reputation amongst the ton was one of a gentle-natured lady who always spoke a kind word to anybody she met. However, what one didn't know was that the duchess should never be crossed. Sophia's hostility rolled off in waves. Phillip slunk in his chair, hoping to make himself so small that Sophia would leave. He would rather have dealt with Sheffield than his wife.

"Why have you called?" Sophia asked.

"Belle."

"I am aware of the reason, I am asking why?"

"I wish to speak to her."

Sophia sighed in annoyance. "There again, I know. Why do you wish to speak with her? Perhaps to offend her again?"

"No."

"To besmirch her name?"

"No." Phillip gritted his teeth.

"To accuse her of harming *your loved ones*?"

"No," he growled.

"Then why, my lord, have you called on Belle?"

"In all due respect, Your Grace, that subject only concerns Belle and I."

"Well, 'tis not possible. I will not allow your visit with Belle."

Phillip ran his hands along his trousers, trying to remain calm. He wanted to shout his frustrations at Sophia, but knew it would only lead to being thrown out.

"I understand your reservations, Phee."

"Phee is only reserved for those I consider a friend. You, my lord, are no longer allowed that privilege. You may refer to me as Your Grace."

It would seem Phillip wouldn't be making an apology to Belle this evening after all. Between Sheffield's torture of having him sit outside in the cold all day, to his wife's utter disdain, he had once again failed. However, before he left, he would impress himself upon Sophia. Phillip would make her see the sincerity of his wishes. That Phillip should be given a chance to prove to Belle's friends that he meant Belle no harm.

"I have come to grovel at her feet. I wish to apologize for my unkind words yesterday."

"Unkind? No, my lord. The words you spoke to Belle yesterday were beyond cruel. They destroyed her."

"It was not my intention. The passion of the moment caused my regretful remarks. I had not yet overcome the fear I felt for my child's welfare."

"That is no excuse."

"You are correct, Your Grace. I humble myself to you, to plead my case. I want to take the pain away that I have caused Belle. Please allow me a few moments with her."

"Can I inquire about some information from you, Lord Delamont?"

Sophia's question confused him. But he realized that he must cater to Sophia's whims if he wished for even a slight chance with Belle.

"What do you wish to ask?"

"During the past few weeks, Belle and you have spent much time alone. Am I correct?"

"Yes."

"During those occasions, did you ever discuss the past?"

"No."

"That explains much. Did it ever occur to you to open the discussion so you could move forward with your relationship? Unless you were only trifling with her affections again and you did not foresee a future with Belle."

"No, I was too much of a coward to admit to my genuine feelings. Also, I was afraid to speak of the past for fear of driving Belle away. I thought, in time, I would convince her of a life together. However, Belle recently made it abundantly clear that she did not trust me. Or in us, for that matter."

"Had you ever given her reason to?"

"At one time, yes."

"You betrayed that trust once before, so can you blame Belle for guarding herself against you?

"No, I cannot," Phillip sighed.

"Why did you slander her character with those insults? Especially the ones regarding Henry?" By this time Sophia was standing over him, the passion of her anger and disappointment taking over. "I urged Belle to start a relationship with you again. Even after I learned of her heartache and pain of losing you all those years ago. I told Belle to give you a second chance, that you appeared sincere in your courtship. But you fooled me the same as you fooled all of her friends. How can you believe she would deliberately bring harm onto your child? She has never harmed any child *of yours*, nor would she ever."

~~~~

Sheffield guided Belle out of his study. He'd updated her on the progress made today at the club. A sense of relief settled over her. On their way to the dining room for dinner, they overheard Sophia's raised voice coming from the tiny parlor in the rear of their home. The anger in Sophia's tone and Belle's worried glance hurried them along. When they arrived outside the door, Belle grabbed Sheffield's arm when she heard Phillip's voice. Sheffield tried to open the door, but Belle stopped him. She shook her head at him to wait.

They listened to the conversation between Sophia and Phillip. Belle smiled at her friend's defense and Sophia's set-downs to Phillip. He wouldn't have expected this behavior from sweet Sophia. But Sophia was never sweet if she had to protect a loved one. However, when she mentioned children, Belle needed Sheffield to interrupt.

"Please stop her, Alex, before she says any more. I am going to my room. I cannot see Phillip yet."

Sheffield watched Belle hurry along the hall and up the staircase. *Yet*. He sighed. Belle didn't say *never*—she said *yet*. Which only meant that she would forgive the scoundrel. Belle may not want Sophia to spill her secrets, and he knew Belle never would. However, the arse deserved to understand the full act of his consequences when he'd first abandoned Belle.

He opened the door. "*My dear*, our guest needs your assistance upstairs."

"I am not finished here, *my dear*."

Sheffield came to Sophia and led her toward the door. "Yes, you are."

"But, Alex—"

"No, Phee."

Sophia growled at him, slamming the door on her way out. Sheffield listened to her angry strides leading away. Damn these people. He would have much to make up to Sophia now later this evening. Much later.

"Thank you, Sheffield."

"I sent my wife away at Belle's request, not because I felt any sympathy for you. You deserved much more from Sophia. You have indeed raised her wrath. Tsk, tsk."

"Bugger off, Sheffield."

"I would gladly, but you see, you are in my home."

Phillip watched Sheffield take great delight in besting him.

"You will not allow my visit with Belle either, will you?"

"Not until Belle relents. She is not yet ready to see you."

"Yet? So that means she will?" Phillip held out hope at that simple three lettered word. *Yet.*

Phillip rose from his seat, wanting to take his leave with this sliver of hope. He started for the door. However, before Phillip could walk out, Sheffield blocked his path.

"Your actions surprise me, Delamont. You degrade Belle and her profession, yet you came to her aid just hours before that. I never realized you held that much clout. I am impressed though. How sad that you could not enjoy the glory of coming to her rescue and being the savior. Instead, you had to shame and accuse Belle of bringing harm to your child." Sheffield leaned forward, his eyes piercing Delamont. Sheffield's next words were spoken slowly, one at a time. Each of them impacting Phillip. *"Belle would never harm any child of yours."*

Not your child. Any child of yours. *"I have never set out to harm any child of yours."* Her words echoed all around him. To Sophia's comment, *"She has never harmed any child of yours, nor would she ever."* Phillip only had one child—and Henry wasn't even truly his. Not physically, anyway. Only where it mattered the most, from the heart. However, these none-too-subtle innuendoes spoke otherwise. Did Belle have his child? If so, where was the child now?

"Did Belle have my child?"

Sheffield nodded.

"A boy or girl?"

"The child was a boy."

Phillip cleared his throat. "Where is the child now?"

Sheffield looked upon him with pity.

Was a boy. Meaning the child no longer lived. Phillip closed his eyes, Belle's pain surrounding him.

"What happened?" Phillip slumped into a chair.

"Belle had a difficult childbirth. Her health suffered when you left her. In despair, she neglected to take care of herself. However, once the babe started moving, she pulled herself out of that depression and strived to take better care. The baby brought light to her darkness. I helped to make plans for their future and even proposed. Belle refused my hand in marriage. She told me that one day I would find my soul mate, as she had found hers, and when I did, she would not be the burden that kept us apart."

"What happened to my baby, Sheffield?"

"Her time came sooner than it should have and Belle lost a lot of blood. The doctor and midwife did not know if she or the child would survive. But Belle was stubborn, and so was the boy. She gave birth to him. However, the child was born too early. The doctor said its lungs were not fully developed. The babe died in Belle's arms. Even though everyone assured her it was not her fault, she blamed herself."

"Oh, Rosalyn." Phillip covered his eyes. He wanted to run and search the house for Belle and hold her close. He wanted to kneel at her feet and beg for forgiveness. But Sheffield was not through with him yet.

"She lost her entire world that day. She lost herself."

"Why are you telling me this now?"

"Because I think you deserve to understand what Belle has endured for loving you. Nothing but pain, heartache, abandonment, and cruelty. And so much more that I cannot even begin to name. You simply want to apologize, but you've never understood the impact of your actions."

"I am beginning to understand."

"No, you are not even close. Rosalyn created Belle because she thought that was all she was worth. You took a simple country maiden who adored you and turned her into a tortured soul who still believes she does not deserve a better life. You forced her into the very life you shame her for. Why? Why did you do that to her? Was it because of the power you gained by marrying your wife? A woman that I, even as your best friend, held no knowledge of. Please explain why."

"Because of my father."

"Your father is dead."

"Yes, but not before he raped an innocent lady and got her with child."

"Henry is not …?"

"Mine? No, although he *is* mine in all that matters. Do you mean, is Henry the product of a union between Julia and myself? No, he is my father's child."

Sheffield was stunned by this news. He had heard rumors of Delamont's father's nefarious ways. Delamont put his own desires to the side for an innocent child. A sacrifice that cost him the woman he loved and a child he knew nothing of.

"Then why did your father not marry the girl?"

"He refused. You know what a cold-hearted bastard he was. Julia's father tried to trap him, using his daughter as bait. When my father had one of his wild, infamous debaucherous parties, her father brought Julia to it. I had come home that weekend, unaware of his entertainments. When I ran into her, I saw her innocence. She tried to remain inconspicuous, but Julia was a rare beauty. Every man in that house noticed her. I tried to protect her. She was a timid miss who liked to read a lot. But her innocent charm did not go unnoticed. When I asked her why she was in attendance, she admitted to me that her father had tricked her into believing the house party would be filled with young ladies she could befriend. Lord Minturn was in my father's debt. My depraved father had met Julia upon calling to collect his markers. When Lord Minturn could not pay, Father convinced the man to bring Julia to his house in the country. Lord Minturn thought my father was interested in *marrying* Julia." Delamont's cynical laughter filled the air.

"However, that was never my father's intention. He is the very reason I never brought Rosalyn around. With one look at her, he would have devoured her. I thought Julia was safe in her room with the door locked, so I left for the night. A night that I spent in Rosalyn's arms. A night I will never forget. It was the night she gave herself to me, the same night I fell deeper in love than I had ever been. When I returned home in the early morning, I knocked on Julia's door to make sure she'd had a peaceful night. I heard a whimpering sound inside. When she would not answer, I turned the knob, although I should never have gone into her room without permission."

Delamont rose and started pacing the small room. The room suffocated him from the very air he needed to breathe. He couldn't remove the horror from his thoughts. Julia beaten, laying naked on the floor, curled into a tight ball. Her body racked with sobs. Delamont remembered trying to touch her and how Julia recoiled in fear. Delamont lifted the blanket off the bed, covering her body. His soft words soothed her. But they didn't stop the tears from falling.

Delamont rubbed the back of his neck.

"She promised me not to tell her father. I had our housekeeper see to Julia's welfare. They left shortly thereafter. My father strutted around, smug with himself. I confronted him and he threatened that Rosalyn would be next if I so much as spoke a word of Julia again. He gloated knowledge of my little secret crush and the pleasure he would take when he crawled between Rosalyn's thighs. In my anger, I attacked him. I felt nothing but rage and disgust for the man who sired me. All he did was laugh."

"That still does not explain why you married the girl."

"When her father discovered Julia's pregnancy, he brought her to our home. My father denied ever sleeping with the girl. He had witnesses, his cronies, to verify that he spent that night playing cards with them. Then he brought the housekeeper in and had her tell Julia's father about my attendance in her room that morning. Since I would not explain my whereabouts for the evening with Rosalyn, and I was inside her bedroom the next morning, then that could only mean that I slept with the girl. My father told Lord Minturn that he would have the banns read and I would marry his daughter. Her father agreed. The housekeeper later confessed how my father threatened her family if she did not agree to his lies. The manipulative bastard ruined so many lives that fateful day. I would not allow an innocent woman to be ruined amongst them, all because of my father."

"So you sacrificed yourself. And for what?"

"For a son I call my own. He is as much an innocent as anybody is to this sad tale."

"And your marriage to Julia? Was that enjoyable?"

"We settled into a comfortable life after my father died. Thankfully, it was not long after we married and before Henry was born. At least he never got to see him. Father made us miserable with his gloating. My greatest revenge came when he lay on his death bed and I got to tell him that he would not see his child for a single day."

"Were you ever going to share this with Belle?"

"I had meant to. Every time I tried, she would distract me, or find something she needed to attend to."

"Those are excuses, Delamont."

"I did not want to relive what lay in the past."

"Yes, but the past always has a way of coming into the present. And stops the future from moving forward.

"How can my future move forward, when she will not even speak to me?"

"You must prove yourself worthy of her."

"How?"

"Delamont, I had to grovel at my wife's feet to gain back her love and trust. You must find your own way, if Belle is the one you want?"

"She is all that I have ever wanted."

"Excellent. Now, if you do not mind, I think it is time for you to take your leave. I have only one suggestion for you."

"And that is?"

"If you truly love her, then do not be afraid to use her weakness against her."

"What is her weakness?"

Sheffield laughed, the man was such a fool. Did he have to draw a picture?

"The boy," Sheffield stressed.

"The boy?" Delamont whispered.

"The boy." Sheffield nodded.

Chapter Fourteen

Phillip wasn't above using his son to win back Belle's hand. He was a man left with no pride, and Phillip planned to use anything and anyone to his advantage to have but a moment of Belle's time. However, her friends shot him down at each attempt. They would intercept his messages or refuse him entry into Sheffield's home. Winning Belle's love wouldn't be easy. Phillip assumed Sheffield was an ally, since he gave him advice. But Sheffield only stood back with a smirk when each woman denied Phillip access. At first he tried not listening to Sheffield's suggestion of using his son. However, when even Henry offered, why should Phillip refuse? So, on his next visit to Sheffield's, he brought along his son. When the women fussed over Henry and informed Phillip to collect him later, his confidence deflated. Didn't these women have homes of their own? His own son had turned traitor for a chance to spend time with Belle, and for delicious treats. Henry's loyalty cost nothing more than a biscuit.

    Phillip headed to his club. He needed a few stiff drinks to help him rethink a plan of attack. There had to be a way to gain access to Belle without her flock of guards. He ordered a brandy, listening to a roar of laughter coming from a private room. At least those blokes were having a swell time. Phillip had the glass to his mouth when a hand slapped him on the back. He choked on the drink, sending it spraying across the bar.

    "Careful now, perhaps you need to be cut off already?"

    "I have yet to enjoy one drink."

"I thought I noticed you slinking through the door. Come join us in Sheffield's private room." Beckwith nodded toward the boisterous area.

"No thanks. I have had enough of His Grace's hospitality for the week."

Beckwith laughed. "Yes, I know what you mean. At one time, I barely tolerated the man. There are still some days I would like to plant my fist on his face again."

"Again?"

"Yes." Beckwith smiled.

"Sounds like there is a story there."

"Sure is, come in the room. I would love to share it."

Phillip sighed, suddenly guessing he was the reason for their laughter. "He is telling stories on how I cannot gain access to Belle."

Beckwith laughed again. "Did you really try to sneak in through the servant's entrance?"

Phillip said wryly, "Yes, not one of my finer moments."

"We have all had those. Come join us."

Phillip followed Beckwith into the private room. The men married to the women protecting Belle sat around the fire, sharing a drink. When he walked in, their laughter started again. Phillip shook his head, wondering why he'd followed Beckwith. He figured he deserved the misery.

"So the boy didn't work?" Sheffield asked.

"He turned traitor for a plate of biscuits and motherly attention. Your wife told him of a book she bought. One that Henry had been wanting for a while. One that I planned to buy him. But no, Sophia tempted him away. I did not even get a chance to set eyes on Belle."

"Yes, Sophia knows how to tempt," murmured Sheffield.

The men in the room groaned.

But their wives were just as guilty as Sophia from keeping him from Belle, and Phillip proceeded to tell them. However, they already knew. He was the very reason they were enjoying themselves earlier. All at his expense.

"Should we put him out of his misery? Maybe offer him some advice?" Wildeburg suggested. "Or should he suffer longer?"

Holdenburg said, "You gentlemen are vindictive. I vote we offer him some advice. I imagine he has suffered enough, and his suffering has lasted longer than ours."

"I agree," said Beckwith.

"Very well," agreed Wildeburg.

All eyes turned to Sheffield. They understood of his protective feelings for Belle. It had to be agreed by all before any of them offered Delamont help.

"I already gave him a suggestion. It is not my fault he did not use the boy effectively."

"Did you try delivering her favorite candy?" Wildeburg asked.

"I do not know what kind she favors."

They all answered, "Cherries dipped in chocolate and cordial."

"I do not even want to know how every single man in this room knows that," Delamont growled.

"Settle down, Delamont. If any of us needed a favor from Belle, we would bribe her with her favorite treat," explained Wildeburg.

"How about a love letter?" Sheffield made another suggestion.

"Your wives would intercept it before Belle could read it."

"Well, you could try sneaking into her room. It worked for Wilde and myself with our wives," Beckwith said.

"Once again, I tried, but Sidney and Dallis both caught me before I even climbed the stairs."

"Amateur. You do not take the stairs in the middle of the day, you fool," said Wilde.

"You sneak in through her windows in the dead of night," Beckwith laughed.

"Not in my house," growled Sheffield.

"Why don't you take Belle somewhere special that holds meaning of your future together and confess your love?" said Holdenburg.

"Seriously, that is the best you can do, Holdenburg? I do not see how my sister fell for you." Beckwith shook his head in disgust.

"Would you like for me to explain how and why your sister fell for me? I do not think you would care for the details."

"Enough, gentlemen." Wilde once again tried to stop a fight before it got out of hand.

Phillip said, "While your suggestions are a bit unorthodox and may have merit, I wish to win Belle on my own terms. And if you would convince your wives to stand down, then perhaps I might have a chance."

They *all* laughed at this. Each man wouldn't go against their wife's wishes. And right now their greatest enjoyment was to make Delamont suffer. If these gentlemen wouldn't convince their wives otherwise, then Delamont would have to create a distraction for each lady until they left Belle alone. Delamont remembered one more friend of Belle's he could ask for help. He didn't understand why he hadn't considered seeking Claire's support before. As each man kept offering ideas, none of them serious, Delamont came up with a plan of his own. One he wouldn't share with them. It ran too much of a risk of them telling their wives.

He would win Belle's hand on his own terms.

With a gentle smile Belle brushed the hair off Henry's forehead. Henry's openness to Belle endeared him to her heart. She would miss him, if she left. She hadn't decided where to go. If Phillip didn't accept her for who she was, there was no need to stay in London. Belle knew Phillip regretted his spiteful words and only spoke them out of fear for his son. When Sheffield explained what had happened all those years ago, it only made her love Phillip more. Phillip had regained her trust. The sacrifices he'd made for the sweet lad laying her in lap was worth the heartache she'd endured.

"Are you going to put the bloke out of his misery soon?" Kathleen asked.

"I have not decided yet."

"In my opinion he has suffered through enough of our ploys," Dallis said.

"Oh, but they've been so entertaining. Especially the time he tried sneaking through the servant's quarters to reach you. I do not think I have laughed so hard in a long time," Sidney chuckled.

Sophia was the only one who didn't comment. She watched Belle, wearing a thoughtful expression. Sophia's anger had calmed once Sheffield shared Phillip's story. However, Sophia had been the one who held Belle through her tears when she first arrived. Her protectiveness was worse than her husband's. Sophia, with her open heart, still feared for any kind of heartache Belle might suffer.

"Phee?" asked Belle.

"Your decision is not for me to decide, it is only for you to make. You are the only one who understands how it will affect your heart, whichever path Phillip chooses. He holds your fate in his hand. Do you trust Phillip with this?" Phee asked.

Belle took a deep breath. Phee said it so eloquently. Did Belle want to give Phillip her heart this one more time? Would Belle survive the pain if he were to reject her again? How much of herself was she willing to give to Phillip? If he didn't want her for a wife and only for a mistress, would that be enough for Belle? Could she spend the rest of her life being at Phillip's beck and call for only when he wanted to spend time with her? Belle looked again at the sleeping child and knew that for Henry, she would agree to whatever decision Phillip would make. To be with Phillip and Henry for only a brief time was better than never being with him at all.

"Ladies, I believe I have made my decision."

They all sat forward eagerly in their chairs. Smiles of anticipation lit their faces. When Belle encountered Sophia's gaze, she saw her caring acceptance of any decision Belle made. Then when Sophia smiled with the same anticipation, Belle's heart felt lighter.

"I think I will allow Lord Delamont to call on me now. However, I will return to my home after today. If I allow him to visit, it will be on my terms, in my home."

"But Belle—" Sidney said.

"Yes, I am aware the place sits empty except for my private quarters. But Lord Delamont does not know this yet. I will inform him I am closed for remodeling. If I am to understand if he accepts me for who I am, then he must not know. The only people who hold knowledge of the closure of my business besides my employees are you ladies and your husbands. My dearest friends. My plans have not changed. If his lordship does not wish to continue our affair, then I will move on with the plans I have made. With your help and assistance, I think we can make our dream come true."

After saying this, they all whispered offers of advice. None of them wished to wake the boy just yet. Some of their comments were most scandalous, and Belle covered Henry's ears just in case he listened. They even made her blush. She, the most notorious Madame in London. However, Belle only listened out of politeness, because she had already planned on how to make Phillip grovel. Belle wouldn't forgive Lord Delamont so easily, and he would have to prove his love.

"Excuse me, Your Grace, but the lad's father awaits in the foyer."

"Please inform his lordship that Henry will come out shortly."

"Henry, it is time to wake, my love. Your papa is here." Belle gently shook his shoulder.

Henry rolled over and looked at the woman he already considered his mama. If only his father would stop blundering in his attempts to seek her forgiveness. Henry still didn't understand why everyone here called her Belle. But it would appear that she had forgiven Papa and would soon let him visit. His Papa thought he had betrayed him today with the offer of biscuits. Well, maybe a little. He'd also pretended to fall asleep, because he liked how Rosie held him and brushed at his hair. When she spoke of allowing Papa to see her again, he listened to the plans. He would tell Papa what he overheard—although for a long time Rosie had held her hands over his ears.

Henry stood and hugged Rosie tight. He feared that if Papa failed with Rosie, he might never see her again. Never have Rosie hold him in her arms while she offered him comfort. Never allowed special treats. Never to talk of his favorite books again.

"Bye, Mama," Henry said, when he ran out the door.

"Mama?" Belle whispered. Henry called her *Mama*. She watched him run away and followed, but came to a halt in the hallway when she saw Phillip.

Phillip looked up at the footsteps following Henry and saw Belle standing a few feet away. He took a step forward, noticing her bewildered expression. She glanced back and forth between him and Henry. With a gasp Belle ran back toward the parlor. Phillip started forward, but Henry tugged at his hand urging them to leave. Caught between comforting the woman he loved and his son, Phillip had to choose Henry for now.

Phillip walked down the sidewalk toward their home with Henry chattering a storm. He didn't listen to one word of what Henry said. Phillip couldn't forget the look upon Belle's face. What did it mean?

"Then Rosie said she is returning home."

At the mention of Rosie, Phillip stopped.

"Rosie is returning home?"

"Yes, Papa. Have you listened to a word I have spoken?"

For only being seven years of age, Henry spoke with the tone of a mature gentleman, disappointed that Phillip hadn't been paying attention.

"No, son. I am afraid my mind has been elsewhere."

"With Rosie? Papa, why do some people refer to her as Belle?"

"That would be a lengthy story I do not think you are old enough to understand."

"Well, if you tell me your story, then I will tell you a story I heard today."

Phillip looked upon Henry with skepticism. "What story might that be, lad?"

"One concerning a beauty named Belle who has forgiven the lord who captured her heart. Only his sword cut her deeply. She will set her dragons free and might be alone in her castle soon."

"Might be left alone?"

Henry shrugged. "I cannot quite remember all the details of the story. However, for a frozen ice I might be able to recall them."

Phillip laughed. Henry was a manipulator for all things sweet.

"I do not know if you deserve a frozen ice. You abandoned me today for biscuits. Why should I reward such treason?"

"Papa, I am but an ally. I only appeared to be a traitor so I could be a spy."

Why the little devil.

"Mmm. A flavored ice you say?"

"Yes, sir."

"And you have intelligence I could use in my plan on winning Rosie's hand?"

"Very secretive information."

Phillip took another path, taking them toward Piccadilly Square for a flavored ice. He finally understood, if he made Belle his wife, the full impact it would have on his son's life. She would be his mother. However, her past could come back to ruin them. While he no longer cared of the ruination, his son could. It would close many doors for him when he grew older. The consequences would harm the family line for eternity. However, without Belle in their lives, it would harm their hearts for the rest of their time on God's earth.

With the flavored ices in hand they settled on a bench in a park nearby. Phillip told Henry the story of how he met Rosie in the past, and how they went their separate ways. He had long ago decided and promised Julia that he would never share Henry's true parentage with him. Phillip explained how, when he met Rosie in London, she had changed her name to Belle and the reason why. He described the full implications of how, if he married Belle, it would bring shame to their family. When Henry came to

Belle's defense and told Phillip that he didn't care as long as Belle became his mother, it was all Phillip needed to hear. Then Henry started referring to Belle as Mama when he reported what he learned during the afternoon tea. Phillip's decision became firm with Henry's devotion toward Belle. Before the week was finished, he would make Belle his wife.

Phillip already carried the special license in his pocket. He had gotten the document the day after his talk with Sheffield. This time Phillip would never let Belle go.

Chapter Fifteen

Belle returned to taking her walks through the park and soon fell back into her routine. Belle had neglected visiting her other friends long enough. Also, she missed the children. Their silly laughs, their constant questions, and watching their fun games. Belle's hands were full today carrying a tin of biscuits. She had many days to make up for.

When she arrived, Claire exclaimed with glee. They fell into their familiar chat as if Belle hadn't disappeared the last few weeks. Claire explained how her mother took the babe for the afternoon, giving her a much-needed break. Ashley crawled on Belle's lap, asking her a million questions. Belle missed these moments. Soon, with a biscuit in hand, Ashley ran after the other children. Before long, the children in the park surrounded Belle, each of them clamoring for a special treat. Belle laughed with delight.

"You spoil the children so," said Claire.

"They are too precious not to be spoiled."

"You will make a wonderful mother one day."

"Those days will never come. The path I chose to walk will prevent me from enjoying those moments in life."

"Fiddlefash."

Belle turned. "Excuse me?"

"You heard me. Fiddlefash. You may have chosen that path, but that path did not choose you."

"You do not understand what you speak."

"Oh, but I do, *Madame*." Claire arched an eyebrow.

Horror flashed across Belle's face. "You know," Belle whispered.

"I have always known, *my lady*."

"But …"

"But how?"

Belle nodded, too choked to speak. She thought she had been so careful all these years. When all along, everyone knew. Belle glanced around the park at everybody she befriended over the years, looking for any sign of disgust directed her way.

"We live in a small word, Rosie. Nobody in this park judges you. They see you for the person you are and the generosity you gifted them with over the years. At first, I was skeptical and guarded my children from you. But your kind words and thoughtfulness overruled any judgmental opinion I held. Everyone watches what you do for our community. For those less fortunate, and for those who need a helping hand along the way. When Lord Delamont started appearing regularly and showed attention to you, every single one of your friends in this neighborhood, and your ones in society, felt joy for you. We encouraged the courtship, wanting you to find the happiness you most deserve. We missed your kind soul and became accustomed to his distraught face. Our greatest hope is for you two to find love together."

Belle was overcome with gratitude at Claire's admissions. She never held a clue and these kind people had never hinted. Their acceptance humbled Belle. Tears slid along her cheeks with a smile. Belle gripped Claire's hands.

"I am so proud to call you my friend," said Claire.

"And I, you, mine," replied Belle.

"And him over there," Claire nodded toward the trees. "Will you please forgive that man? His misery is a most depressing sight to watch day in and day out. He waits here every day hoping you will come." Claire laughed.

"Yes, I plan to," said Belle, staring at Phillip leaning against a tree. He didn't attempt to come over, and Belle didn't offer any encouragement. "But not now. Would you be a kind friend and give him this letter when I leave? It will explain all to him."

Belle rose and handed the letter to Claire. She smoothed her skirts. With a brief glance over one shoulder Belle sent Phillip a smoldering gaze, portraying her feelings. With a thank you to Claire, she walked away. Belle strolled along the path that had been a source of comfort whenever she needed to feel normal. Along the way she returned the acknowledgements, noting the genuine smiles on their faces. While Belle had always felt like a lost soul floundering in life, believing that nobody cared for her, friends were always right in front of her eyes. These people had become her family.

~~~~~

Phillip pushed himself off the tree, striding across the open lawn towards Belle. When he reached the bench Claire stood and placed a hand on the front of his suit. Phillip glanced down and back to her face, arching his eyebrows. She stood firm. A lord's disdain wouldn't deter Claire—not that he held any. Phillip didn't want Belle to slip through his fingers again. He'd come so close today. When Belle sent him a smoldering stare, he wanted to run after her and throw Belle over his shoulder.

"Belle wanted me give you this letter, Lord Delamont."

Claire waved a letter between them. When he tried to grab it, she stepped away from him and hid the letter behind her back. Claire sat back down, holding the envelope on her lap, fingers curled around the paper, taunting him with Belle's words.

Phillip slumped down on the bench, seeing Belle had left the park. Claire watched Belle leave too and then handed him the letter. He rose to follow. If he ran, he could catch her. But once again, Claire prevented him, tugging on the sleeve of his coat suit.

"What?" he growled.

Claire only laughed. "Read the letter, Lord Delamont. Belle wanted me to tell you she explained her wishes in the note. She does not wish for you to follow her at this time."

"But she wishes for me to follow her at another time?"

"She did not confide in me that, but I believe so."

"Did you tell her what we discussed?"

"Yes, my lord, It brought me much joy to lighten her burden."

"You are a dear friend, Claire."

"As you are, Lord Delamont."

"Phillip."

Claire smiled at his generous offer. "Phillip."

~~~~~

Phillip waited throughout the day to read Belle's letter. He wanted to rip it open right in the park, but didn't want any witnesses. He didn't know if Belle was ending their relationship by ink and paper, or if she wished for more. Either way, Phillip required no audience. Once he returned home, Phillip encountered one visitor after another. Since his return to London, his townhouse hadn't seen this much company. Every single one of Belle's friends called on him during the day. Each on a separate occasion as if they were playing a game at his expense. Were they trying to keep him away from Belle? Some of them came by themselves, other times they would come as husband and wife. They timed it so Phillip wouldn't have a moment to spare to read Belle's missive.

The last visitors of the day were Sheffield and Sophia. Henry joined them in the parlor when he learned Sophia had come to visit. Henry enjoyed having Sophia spoil him. Sophia and Henry read from his favorite book, while Sheffield droned on and on about political debates or the historical antiquities that he funded with Lord Hartridge. Each subject grated on Phillip's nerves, one right after the other. Phillip longed to read Belle's words. When were they ever going to leave? They stayed past the fashionable hour for tea. But one did not ask a duke and duchess of the realm to leave before they were ready. Phillip sat with his foot tapping in annoyance and his fingers drumming against the chair handles while Sheffield continued to prattle on. It was only when Sheffield paused and Phillip heard the laughter in Sheffield's voice when he began discussing his newest business venture that Phillip realized it was all a ploy. This entire day *had* been on purpose. From the time he left the park to this every instant. When Phillip glared at him, Sheffield returned a nod of approval. It appeared all of Belle's friends assisted in, and approved of, Belle's decision.

Sheffield rose and urged Sophia of their need to leave, reminding her of a previous engagement. With a promise to Henry to return another day, they took their leave. When Phillip thought he would have a few moments to read the letter, the butler announced dinner. Phillip ate dinner with Henry, only half-listening to the praise of Sophia and her kindness. The letter burned a hole in his pocket. After they ate, Henry wished to play a game of chess, and Phillip couldn't refuse the boy for his own selfish reasons. Phillip understood the letter was only a beginning. A beginning not to be rushed.

However, with his calm acceptance of yet another delay, Phillip still had trouble concentrating. He kept wondering what to expect. So much so, he hadn't paid attention to the game until Henry announced checkmate. Phillip look down at the board and realized he had nowhere to move.

"Well done, Henry."

Henry smiled but didn't gloat for besting his Papa. He started to put the pieces away and then paused, for he needed to admit to his betrayal. Mama had made it clear to him to be a diversion for a few hours after the Duke of Sheffield and his wife left. Only long enough for a plan to come to fruition. She didn't want Henry to lie to Papa.

"Papa, do you remember when I told you I was not an ally but a spy?"

Phillip sat back smiling, amused. "Yes, I remember."

"Well, I must admit the circumstances changed and I became a double agent. One for my papa and one for my mama."

Phillip raised his eyebrow. "Is that so?"

"Yes, but Mama promised it was for the good of the family that I betray you this evening."

"And how were you to betray me?"

"By keeping you occupied until my bedtime hour."

The clock chimed behind them announcing that time.

"Well, you achieved your orders. What is your next move?"

"I am to wish you good evening and go to bed after I admitted to my deception."

"Were there any further instructions?"

"Yes, I am to tell you to read the letter you received today. Then you are to follow the instructions that Mama wrote."

Phillip nodded. "Then let us get you to bed with undue haste. It would appear I must complete my own mission."

Henry smiled, taking off at a run toward his bedroom. He got ready for bed in a hurry, crawling under the covers. Phillip reached down and tucked him in. He gave him a kiss on the forehead, something he had not done since Henry was a small child.

"Papa, will Mama be here when I awake in the morning?"

"I will not be returning until your mama is by my side. I hold no clue on how long it will take, but I will not accept no for an answer."

"It is my belief Mama does not plan on saying no." Henry yawned, closing his eyes.

~~~~~

Phillip stood staring out the window with the letter held in his hand. His fingers shook unfolding the worn paper. Her delicate penmanship leapt off the page. Phillip looked out the window again, too nervous to read the words. Every sign today pointed in the direction that Belle had forgiven him and wanted him to return. However, he'd lost her before and it was the fear of never holding Belle in his arms again that kept him from reading. He sat down in the chair near the lamp and stared upon the paper. With a deep breath, Phillip began to read.

My darling Phillip,

I do not know where to begin. One would say from the beginning, but I do not think it would work in our case. Throughout the lifetime of our relationship we have not trusted in our love. I think that is why we have had our recent misunderstanding. It was not because I did not trust in you and you did not trust in me. It is because we did not trust in the love we shared.

I know I have not uttered those words since your return. It ached too much to speak them. I feared if I did, those simple words would have too much control over me. You, yourself never uttered those words, except to call me your love. Which to me were only words of devotion not the simple act itself. I had heard those words uttered too many times over the years, by the gentleman calling on my girls, to really know what the terms were for those words. I understand you may have meant more with your words, but I did not have enough faith in them.

Also, we have both kept secrets from one another. Never sharing the heartache that had kept us apart all these years. We have only learned of them because of Sheffield. A man who means more to me than a friend. One that means the same to you too. I hope we can discuss our heartache and pain together. The only way for us to heal is to speak what we hold dear in our heart.

You need to understand I love your son as much as you do. Henry is a precious child who has helped to heal my heart over these past few weeks. I thank you for allowing me to build a relationship with him. I have never meant him harm nor do I ever wish to bring shame onto him. Whatever you decide I will understand.

I will finish with a request from you. I feel we have much more to share than what I can say in a letter. If you wish, you may call on me this evening. I have returned home from my stay with Sheffield and Sophia. We can decide together on how to proceed with our affair. But be prepared, my lord, I will take no mercy upon your heart and soul.

Your devoted lover,

Rosalyn

Phillip closed his eyes at the sweet words. Hope wrapped itself around his heart. He stared down again at how she signed her name. Not Belle. Not Rosie. But Rosalyn. The name that spoke of her true character. The woman he fell in love with all those years ago, and the woman he would love for the remainder of his days.

He rose and hurried down the stairs. With a few instructions for Henry's welfare, Phillip rushed to be with Belle. He ran to the stables and saddled a horse himself. When he arrived at Belle's home, a shroud of darkness cloaked the house. All except for one section, her private quarters. Phillip ran to the door and read the "Closed for renovations" sign. That explained the quiet. When he turned the knob, the door opened. This made him furious. It would appear he must speak to Belle of the danger of not locking her doors. How could she be so foolish? Phillip stormed along the hallway, throwing the door to Belle's private chamber open. What awaited him almost brought him to his knees.

There on the bed, wearing nothing but a small scrap of lace, lay Belle. Her fiery strands spread across the silk sheets, her body in a provocative pose. Belle shifted on the bed, and the negligee rose higher along her thighs giving him a peek of hidden desires. Her breasts spilled forth, nipples teasing him to take a step closer. Mirrors of all shapes and sizes surrounded the bed and walls. Phillip remembered his wish he asked of Belle. She'd remembered too. Phillip ached to have Belle watch him make love to her. He wanted her to see her reaction when he exploded inside her. When Belle shifted again, exposing her delights, Phillip advanced and tore off his clothing. He would have her now. Phillip could wait no longer to make Belle his again.

Chapter Sixteen

Belle waited in anticipation for Phillip. Not as the naïve maiden with news to share, but as a confident woman who would get what she most desired. And that was Phillip. It had always been him and always would be. Every ounce of pain Belle endured through these last few weeks and years floated away the second Phillip opened the door. The love reflected in his eyes spoke from his heart to hers.

When Phillip strode across the room discarding his clothes, Belle rose and met him at the edge of the bed. They spoke no words. There were no need for them. Phillip swept her into an embrace, devouring her lips with a passionate kiss. Belle wrapped her arms around him, pulling Phillip closer. Her need to touch him would no longer be denied. She wanted to be his again. To feel the love only Phillip could gift her.

Holding Belle's curvaceous body fueled Phillip's desire, his fears vanishing. Her warm response invaded his soul. Phillip's kisses lowered to Belle's neck, breathing in her scent. He whispered, "My sweet Belle." Phillip pulled on her hair, and Belle's body arched into him. Her nipples brushed across his chest. Phillip grew harder and pressed himself into Belle's core. He wanted to take this slow and worship her, even though his body demanded otherwise.

Phillip pulled his lips from Belle's delectable body and watched his fingers trail to her breasts. The scrap of lace caressed her nipples. Phillip drew the fabric away and lowered his head to draw the hardened pebble between his lips. His teeth gently scraped the bud, before sucking the delectable treat. When Belle moaned her pleasure, Phillip slid his hand down between her thighs. At one touch of her warmth, he didn't know how much longer he could last.

Phillip lifted his head and stared upon Belle. She was a vision to behold. A goddess with her head held back, her beautiful globes glistening by the candlelight, and his fingers sunk into her wetness, stroking her desires. Belle was a woman who needed to be loved. Her eyes spoke volumes. She hadn't uttered a word. However, the trust she bestowed upon Phillip with her gaze shined like a beacon of light. He could no longer wait.

With one swift thrust, Phillip entered Belle. Her wetness surrounded him, clinging tight. He paused at Belle's gasp. Phillip never once looked away from her. Belle's eyes drifted closed then reopened with a smoky gaze of desire. Her look was all it took to claim Belle as his again. He pressed his hardness into her core, before slowly pulling out. At her moan of disappointment, he entered her swiftly again. This time harder. Her eyes widened at the pleasure. Soon, Belle drew her knee higher around his waist. Her body wrapped around him with each stroke.

Belle was powerless in Phillip's grasp. At his first touch, Belle had been lost. Lost to the emotions Phillip brought to the surface. Lost in his kisses. Lost in the depth of his gaze. She saw his fears and insecurities. She also saw his need. Her body responded to his need. He teased her with only a sampling of what she most desired. When Phillip paused, gazing into her eyes, Belle bestowed him with a look speaking from her heart. Her stare was all that it took.

The passion Phillip breathed into her body shook Belle. The emotions coursing through her were more powerful than anything ever experienced before. Each time he entered her, he gave her a piece of his soul. Belle lifted her hips with every stroke, demanding more. She wanted everything. His every desire. His heart. His soul.

They moved as one, each in perfect rhythm with the other. When the passion grew higher and out their control, they only clung tighter. Each one of them holding on, afraid of letting go. They both still held onto the fear of losing the love they again shared. Their lovemaking became desperate, their passion drawing them to newer heights. They hovered on the brink, lost to the unknown when the depth of their love for one another sent them over the edge. Belle and Phillip held on to each other, floating in the aftermath of their desires. Contentment took hold and settled into their embrace.

No words of love or apologies needed to be spoken.

~~~~

Belle drifted back to the reality of the moment. Her seduction plans for Phillip had flown out the window. Never had their attraction sizzled as it had once he opened the door to her bedroom. Even now her body craved for him again. She would never be able to get enough of Phillip. Belle thought she'd convinced herself that if Phillip only wanted her body, it would be enough. But she was wrong. She wanted so much more. Belle wanted Phillip to love her unconditionally.

Belle stirred in Phillip's arms, making him realize his plan to make right by Belle didn't come to scratch. He'd meant to apologize to Belle and declare his love before bedding her. However, all it took was the vision of her loveliness calling to him. Belle's siren's call would always be his demise. Now Phillip needed to turn his failure into a love she couldn't refuse. He would now set out to show Belle how much she meant to him. Words could wait. They would share a lifetime together for him to whisper every day how much she meant to him. Now he would only love her.

Phillip rolled over Belle, staring into her dreamy gaze. He drew her lips into a slow sensuous pleasure. His tongue stroked hers into a slow dance. Their kisses drawing from one another. When Phillip heard Belle's moan of desire, he pulled away. His gaze drifted down her body, the negligee twisted around her hips. Phillip slid the straps down over her creamy shoulders, pulling the silk away from her breasts, laying her bare to his gaze. Phillip caressed her womanly curves with his eyes, bringing forth a blush to cover Belle from head to toe. While Belle may have presented herself as an experienced woman to her club, she was anything but. She was still a sweet girl arousing to the pleasure of the flesh. A pleasure he would enjoy showing through their lifetime together, if she became his wife.

Phillip's hand slid Belle's legs apart, climbing higher. When he reached his destination, it was to find Belle already wet for him again. He slid two fingers inside, stroking her flames. His thumb pressed against her clit, rubbing the glistening dew back and forth until she tightened around him. Phillip hungered for a taste of Belle. He began to lower his head when Belle pulled at him.

"Phillip," Belle whispered.

"Shh, love. I will ease your ache."

Belle was ready for Phillip again and needed him to fill her. She wanted him inside her. Belle needed to feel herself lost in him. However, Phillip meant to torment her with the stroke of his tongue. Slowly sliding over her wetness, each stroke more demanding, Phillip drew out her passion with each drop. Her ache consumed her. Belle pulled Phillip's head to her core, pressing her wetness to his mouth. Phillip devoured her with each flick of his tongue, to each stroke of his finger, and Belle unraveled.

Belle came undone and Phillip drank from her, craving more. He kept up his ministrations, drawing Belle's passion higher. Phillip demanded, and she gave into him. He slid his tongue in and out of her tight wet core, not relenting, knowing she had more to give. It would never be enough. As his mouth drew out her need, his fingers stroked her clit, adding to the passion. When Belle screamed his name, exploding around Phillip, he calmed her shaking body with tender kisses. He pressed his lips up her body, his caresses light. Phillip drew her breasts in his hands, lowering his head and loving them.

Once again, Belle floated on the aftermath. His lips sought her in a gentle kiss, drawing her into an embrace and holding her tenderly. When Belle sighed her comfort, Phillip chuckled. With a frown Belle rolled above him and noticed a confident man who sought and conquered. Belle had allowed Phillip to gain control over her domain. Well, he may have thought he won, but now Belle would have Phillip begging for her love and forgiveness. She would dominate his senses. Belle narrowed her gaze into a glare.

Phillip paused. His laughter seemed to infuriate Belle. What line did he cross now? Did he mistake her pleasure for more than what he thought? Belle rose above him, sliding her body over him. Phillip grabbed at Belle's arm, trying to pull her back. She shook him off. Phillip dropped his hands, not wanting to pressure her. However, he soon realized Belle's true intentions. She meant to torment him. Belle settled with her legs straddling him, her hot wet core pressing into him. Her body wiggled into position, stroking his cock against her wetness. Phillip closed his eyes groaning. Oh, sweet hell. When he opened his eyes again, he found a devious smile lighting Belle's face. Her hands drifted across his chest, stroking the flames of desire.

Belle laughed softly. Yes, now she had Phillip right where she wanted him. In her control. She would tempt him into begging for her.

While she didn't hold the experience of the girls working for her, they had shared enough stories over the years for Belle to know how to drive Phillip wild. Belle's hand drifted off Phillip's chest and moved to hers. She lifted her breasts, caressing them. Belle pulled at her nipples, twisting them into tight buds. She watched Phillip's eyes darken. She shifted on his hardness, drawing out another groan.

Belle's devious smile turned to one of enjoyment while she teased him. He now understood what she had planned. She meant to make him suffer by drawing out his passion as he had done hers. A suffering he would endure with pleasure. When she slid a hand down to her wetness, he almost spent himself. Belle's fingers slid over his cock in a teasing fashion, stroking him against her. Phillip tried to slide his hand to join hers, but Belle shook her head.

"No, my lord, 'tis my turn now."

What Belle did next would cause Phillip to lie still while she controlled him. Phillip watched Belle dip her fingers into her wetness, coating her fingers. Then she brought them to her breasts, sliding the wetness across the nipples. Little beads of dew hung from the tight perches, ready to drop. Belle leaned forward, holding her breasts above Phillip. She brushed her nipples across his lips. Each time Phillip tried to draw them in or lick at them Belle would pull away. A single dew dropped on his lips. Phillip opened his mouth for more and Belle didn't deny him. She allowed him to draw in the tight buds and lick the wetness away. When he sucked harder, she tsked at him and pulled away. He got too greedy.

She slid her body down, lying between his thighs. Belle's fingers brushed along the length of his cock. Her thumb circling the tip, brushing his dew back and forth. Her hand encircled the strength to hold him in her grip. A groan rumbled from Phillip. Belle raised her head to smile at him when she bent her head to slide her tongue along his hardness. Her tongue circled the head, tracing back and forth. Her lips slid over and softly sucked. Belle hungered for the taste of Phillip. Her mouth glided over his length, pulling him deeper. Belle stroked Phillip in and out of her mouth. Her tongue savoring his length with each pull. Phillip grew harder, which enflamed Belle's desire more. When Phillip's hands gripped her head and guided her, Belle grew wetter, aching for his cock. Belle licked more of his wetness from the tip and knew Phillip was close to exploding. She rose and slid Phillip inside her. Belle closed her eyes and arched her back, moving in slow circles. She felt Phillip in the deepest part of her core. Belle rocked back and forth drawing out each sensation of pleasure.

"Belle," Phillip moaned.

Once Belle placed her sweet lips on his cock, Phillip no longer knew his surroundings. He was at her mercy. Oh, what a carnal mercy it was. Once Belle slid his cock deep inside her pussy, he landed in heaven again. When she rose to slide him out, Phillip protested with a groan. However, Belle wasn't finished with her revenge. With one swift move, she slid back down on him. Deep. Hard. Phillip grabbed her hips, holding on for life as Belle rode him. Her momentum caused her breasts to sway, teasing him. Phillip gave her complete control. Complete control to bring them to ecstasy together.

Phillip's trust in Belle undid her. Throughout her torment, he never once tried to exert control. He let her seek revenge for his brutish behavior. She wanted to show him, that she could be an experienced woman who would be available for his pleasure. Instead Phillip showed Belle his acceptance. Tears slid from her eyes. He'd showered her with his love since he had walked through the door. Phillip broke down the last wall in her defense.

Phillip rose toward Belle. He slid his thumb across her cheek, wiping the tears away. While holding her cheek, he brushed his lips across hers.

"I love you, my sweet Belle."

Phillip sat up, bringing Belle's legs to wrap around him and slid to the back of the bed against the pillows. He held Belle while she cried her sorrow. For their past, for the empty years without each other, and for their present. Phillip whispered words of his love, holding her close, until Belle drifted to sleep.

Phillip held Belle while she slept. He finally understood the full impact of Belle's heartache. He had thought Belle was strong all those years ago and would find a way to move on. Phillip had misjudged the depth of Belle's love. Even now, her love humbled him. When she awoke, Phillip would make sure Belle understood the depth of his love.

Chapter Seventeen

Phillip glided his fingers through Belle's fiery strands. He should let her sleep, but he was a selfish bastard. What remained of his patience to start their life together burned with the candles. He brushed the strands of hair from her face, hoping to waken Belle. When her eyelids fluttered open and love shone from her eyes, his nerves soothed. Phillip brushed his lips across Belle's.

Belle noticed Phillip's nervousness. Belle laced her fingers with his, hoping to ease his distress. She brought them to lie across her stomach. Phillip stared down at them, a frown taking over his features. He untwined his fingers, closed his eyes in pain, and lowered his head to her stomach. Soon his tears flowed, and Phillip's own heartache seeped into Belle's soul. A heartache while shared years apart, still suffered.

He wept over their lost child.

Phillip came to terms with how abandoning Belle caused her to lose their child. Now, he only hoped he could gain her forgiveness. If she didn't forgive him, he didn't see how they would move forward. And Phillip would do whatever he needed to until Belle did. However, Belle didn't make him wait.

"Phillip, look at me," Belle said.

"Please forgive me," Phillip whispered.

"Oh, my love. I forgave you a long time ago. Now, you need to forgive yourself."

It would take Phillip a long time to forgive his own sins.

"Why did you not come to me?"

Belle's laugh was bitter.

"Oh, but I did. Once I came out of my stupor of trying to convince myself that it was all a dreadful dream, I went to your estate. Your father took great pleasure in explaining how I was your summer distraction. He described your happiness with your bride to be. He painted a picture of the future *he* held for you, one that did not include my presence. Your father even extended an invitation to your wedding and encouraged my attendance. I came to the church and watched you take your vows. When I observed your protective behavior toward Lady Julia, I realized your father spoke the truth. Your attentions toward me were false, only for your pleasure and nothing more."

"They were never that, my love. My feelings for you then and now are more powerful than anything I can explain. The day that I lied to you is a day I will always regret. I should have trusted in our love to tell you the truth. Instead I convinced myself you were better off without me."

"But in the end, it would not have changed how our lives played out," said Belle.

Phillip knew Belle spoke the truth. No matter how many times he'd convinced himself otherwise, he still would have married Julia. The torment Julia suffered at his father's hand became his responsibility. A responsibility which gave him a child, while Belle lost theirs.

"Why did you turn to Sheffield?" Phillip's jealously still held strong.

Belle laughed, causing Phillip's frown to deepen. "Oh my love, I did not run into Sheffield's arms."

"His possessiveness of you speaks otherwise. I notice his formidable influence in your life by every decision you make. No, your relationship with Sheffield is more than friendship. The entire time I courted you, Sheffield stewed in envy. He wanted you and pounced on your vulnerability. He could not wait to make you his. And to think he acted the concerned friend when I married Julia. He called me all sorts of a fool for abandoning you and tried to discover why I would pass you over for a miss he never heard of. I should have known he'd chase after your skirts."

Belle pulled back at Phillip's tone. He still besmirched her character when he ranted about Sheffield's act of friendship. Belle rose from the bed, pulling on a robe. She strode across the room, her anger building with every step. When she turned to stalk back toward the bed, her voice rose with each word.

"Court me? You never tried to *court* me. Did you call upon my parents and request their permission for my time? No, I think not. Pssh, court me. Do you not mean, trifle with my affections? No, my lord, you set your sights to seduce me with your whispered words of love and had me worshipping at your feet. Once I fell into your trap, you took my innocence and destroyed what I thought love was. I loved you, Phillip Delamont. When you took my virginity, I loved your gentleness. I loved your playfulness. I loved when you were serious. I loved every aspect of you. I even believed you loved me too. All these years, I held onto that love. Never once letting another man make me his. I loved you upon your return. I love you even now when you are so dim-witted not to understand the love I hold for Sheffield. You cannot even look past your own sense of selfishness to see what is before your eyes."

Belle's angry tirade should have made Phillip see reason. But her mention of holding love for Sheffield only made Phillip see green. Jealousy fueled his next outburst.

"How can you hold love for a man who exploited your relationship into this ... *lifestyle?*" Phillip meant her business.

"The same way I hold love for you. Sheffield did not lead me into this business, but your abandonment did."

"How so?" Phillip snarled.

"Sheffield has never been anything but a friend. And *only* a friend. He called on me soon after your wedding. I broke down and confided my dilemma. Sheffield offered for my hand, but I refused. I could not ruin his life when he had yet to meet his soulmate. Before he left, Sheffield made me a promise that he would return within the week with a solution. Before Sheffield could return, your father discovered my secret and exploited it to his advantage. He spread a rumor through the village of my loose behavior and how I grew heavy with a bastard. My family was shunned by all. My father's angry words and my mother's tears still echo. I had ruined my family, and my sisters were now pariahs who would never gain husbands. The shame I brought upon my family is something I will carry forever. That night my mother packed my bags and my father escorted me to London. His disgust toward me is ingrained in my character, a part of who I am today. He abandoned me just as you had. I made a promise to myself that day that no man would ever hold any power over me. And no man ever has. Nor will they ever."

The more Phillip listened, the angrier he became. Not at Sheffield, or even his father. But at himself. However, as much as his disgust for himself grew, he needed to hear more. He needed to learn the rest of Belle's horrid tale. He wanted the truth.

"Sheffield told my father," Phillip said.

"Yes. You see, Sheffield went to inform *you* of my condition, but your father angered Sheffield into betraying my secret to him. Your father must have been a very convincing man, because he assured Alex that he would secure my future. Alex left there, confident that I would be taken care of. Little did Alex realize at the time, we both were pawns in your father's game of life. When Alex called on me again, my mother told him of my journey to London to wed a gentleman of great esteem. An excuse given to him and the village to explain my absence. Alex left, feeling a sense of relief that your father held true on his promise."

"You still have not explained Sheffield's companionship."

"Yes, well I met him here." Belle swept her hands around at the brothel.

Phillip's hand tightened into fists, his fingers gripping the bedsheets. Belle laughed when she noticed him trying to control his anger, and baited him with her next words.

"Ah, yes, Sheffield. My knight in shining armor who rescued me from my demise. I will forever owe him a debt of gratitude."

When Phillip didn't respond, Belle brushed a lock of hair from his forehead. Her fingers trailed to his cheek, offering him a touch of comfort. Phillip closed his eyes. He would never understand how Belle forgave so easily. Even now, through her own anger, she offered him her love. Phillip didn't deserve her. When he opened his eyes, Belle's wistful smile took hold of his heart and squeezed.

Belle turned away, strolling around, touching the treasures in the room. She became lost in the past, recalling memories that were best forgotten. Memories she had buried long ago. Memories that needed to be spoken for her to move forward. Memories she needed to share with the man she loved.

"Sheffield came to visit the brothel a few months later. The girls were all a twitter on who he would choose to warm his bed. His prowess was the talk of London, and with his return to the city, they knew he would be a regular visitor once again. However, his visit would disappoint the girls."

"How so?"

"The Madame who owned the brothel before me knew of Sheffield's involvement in my abandonment. Upon his arrival she sent for me to meet her in the parlor. I thought nothing uncommon in a request to join her for tea. When I passed Madame in the hallway, she told me to make myself comfortable, and she would be back soon. I entered the parlor, eager to enjoy the comfort of the luxurious sofa to rest my aching backside, and I noticed a man standing with his back to the room. The shock of coming into contact with one of Madame's gentlemen callers sent me making a hasty retreat."

"You lived in a brothel. You would have had daily contact with the clientele. If you did not make your living spreading your thighs, what other employment did you perform? I doubt if a Madame offered tea to a maid."

"The Madame employed my services as a tutor. I educated her girls during the day. Madame understood the more intelligent her ladies were, the more that influential gentlemen of the ton would frequent her establishment. If she offered ladies trained in pleasure, and who also kept her clientele stimulated with titillating conversation, she knew the rooms would stay full every night. She knew how to exploit people to her advantage."

"She was unscrupulous."

"I learned a lot from her. My father left me abandoned in a city I had never visited. Madame took me in, offering me her home. She only did what she had to do, to survive."

"And Sheffield?"

"Yes, Sheffield." Belle smiled, remembering Sheffield's shock at her pregnant form trying to flee the room. "Once Sheffield realized how his actions had led to my suffering, he took it upon himself to take care of me. He called every day, bringing trinkets, flowers, or candy to cheer me. Every girl should have been jealous of the attention he bestowed upon me, but instead they encouraged his visits. They all dreamed of a duke whisking the lowly peasant girl away to his castle and showering her in love. They were all romantics at heart. However, I turned his proposals down every day. When my time grew near, I grew more depressed."

Belle paused. The pain washing over her. Her voice caught, coming out ragged. "I ached for you. I needed your arms to wrap me in your embrace and whisper reassurance in my ears. My labor came early; the babe was in a hurry to come into the world. Our babe," Belle whispered.

Phillip pulled Belle into his arms. He held her through the pain. Phillip murmured the words he should have then, and did so now. He made promises that he would keep.

"The babe was stillborn. I never got to hear him cry. He never cried, Phillip."

"Shh, Belle."

"I held him for a few hours before they took him away. Sheffield made arrangements. He gave the baby a proper burial and paid for a cemetery plot with a stone."

"What did you name the child?"

"Phillip."

"Ah love. Will you take me to him?"

In the effort to comfort Belle, Phillip held himself back from his own emotions. The loss of their child affected Phillip as deeply as it did her. Belle's heart continued to heal while she shared her pain.

"Yes, tomorrow we shall visit him."

Phillip drew Belle's lips under his, kissing with a gentleness he had never shown before. Belle knew Phillip still wanted to understand about Sheffield's influence in her life. She pulled away, needing to finish her tale so he could tell his. Then they could decide on their future together.

Belle continued her story. "Sheffield came every day, offering his friendship. With each day, I became more despondent. But he never gave up. Then a few months after little Phillip's death, Madame became ill. Her sudden death woke me from my stupor. The fear of the unknown awoke my need to survive. The entire time of my depression, the Madame never turned me out of her home, even though I no longer spent my days educating her girls. Everyone in the house cared for me. I realized they were my family. With Sheffield's assistance, he helped me to purchase the brothel. Over the years, with a few shrewd investments, I paid Sheffield back with interest and grew my establishment into the glory it is today. Sheffield's friendship and encouragement is why I love him. Because of him, he gave me a reason to survive. Even with his marriage to Sophia, it has never wavered. They are my family too."

Chapter Eighteen

"I owe Sheffield an apology."

"I believe so," Belle smirked.

Phillip sat on the edge of the bed. Sheffield had hinted at a part of Belle's life after he abandoned her, but Phillip held no clue to the depth of her survival. Because of Phillip's actions, Belle lost everyone in her life. In the scope of things, she lost her entire life as she knew it. All because of the dealings of an evil man. His father's selfish act set a chain reaction of events affecting multiple people—except for himself. His father's life never altered. Belle suffered the most. Yet, she fought against it, to become the woman she was today. Along the way, she never lost who Rosalyn was, she only became a stronger version. No matter what name she went by, she was every one of those ladies rolled into one spectacular woman. Could this creature find it in her heart to forgive him too?

"Rosalyn?"

"Yes, my love?"

"Is it possible for you to find it in your heart to forgive me?"

Belle watched Phillip while he struggled, listening to how her life played out through the years. He hadn't known the lengths of his father's cruelty, Sheffield's kindness, or his own selfishness. Even though Phillip handled his departure from her life in a cruel fashion, he only did so because of another. Phillip spent the last few years paying the price for another's sins. For that alone, there was nothing to forgive. His actions made Belle proud. Phillip gave a child a chance to live an innocent life. Henry was able to grow up surrounded by security and love.

"I forgave you years ago."

"Why?"

"Because you gave me the gift of your love, if only for a short while. Through the years, I realized the difference between love and lust. What we shared was love, and I was lucky to have enjoyed the emotion. I suppose, I always held out hope you would return to me one day."

"And when I did, I ruined that too."

Belle laughed. "Yes, you did at that."

Phillip smiled at Belle's laughter. There was still hope for him yet. "Is there any chance you can also forgive me for the cruel words I spoke a few weeks ago?"

Those words had hurt Belle the most. They were remarks which made Belle doubt her character. Making her feel unworthy. Unrespectable. Dirty. They reminded Belle of Phillip's father. However, it was Belle who allowed those words to have an impact. She gave them the power to hurt her. Those were not the statements of a man who looked down upon Belle, they were the reactions of a man scared for a son he loved. Phillip had only responded from the fear of the unknown. Still, he struck out with words that held some truth. Belle was in a profession she didn't need to be in, and because of her affairs it caused Henry harm. If Belle weren't a brothel owner who made powerful enemies, and if Phillip hadn't become entangled with her, then Phillip would never have set out to destroy Velden. Therefore, Henry would never have been in danger. A complicated mess that should have never come to light. Belle knew of the dangers when she entered into an affair with Phillip. He hadn't understood the complications that would arise.

Phillip waited in silence. It would seem Belle didn't forgive him. Then why the letter inviting him to her home? Why did she allow him to make love to her these past few hours? Was this her idea of revenge?

"Can you forgive yourself?" asked Belle.

"Never."

"Then why should I forgive you?"

Phillip had no answer.

"Why should I forgive a man who degraded me for the fear of his son? Why should I allow him into my life again, fearing that at any moment he might cast me aside with his poor opinion of my character? Should I allow you that power?"

Fear kept Phillip silent. Her questions were valid. Questions he should answer her with reassurances. However, his shame toward degrading her still consumed him. Phillip would never be able to forgive himself, so he should never have expected Belle to do that either.

"Phillip, please look at me." The desperation in Phillip's gaze shook Belle. "Part of loving another leaves you open to being vulnerable. There are times when hurtful words are spoken because of a character's hatefulness. Then there are the instances when they are spoken out of misunderstanding. Of not realizing the full story. Your angry remarks were not spoken because you are a vindictive man, but because you love your son and you feared for Henry's safety. I believe you also spoke them out your fear of our love. I forgive you, Phillip, but you must also forgive yourself. I love you. I always have and I always will. No matter what our future holds."

"I love you, Rosalyn. You were my first love and my only love. I will always regret those words. One day, I might forgive myself, but for now I cannot."

Belle nodded in understanding.

"Do you love me enough to become my wife, and a mother to Henry?"

"We must discuss a few issues before I can decide on a question that complex." Belle smiled impishly. She walked over to him, standing between his legs.

Phillip stared into Belle's eyes, hope flaring. "And what might those be, my love?" Phillip asked, tugging on the belt around her waist.

Belle swatted at his hand. "First and the most important, it concerns Henry. I do not wish to subject your son to ridicule due to my character. I am sure this is not what his mother would have wished."

Phillip slid the knot loose. "I had a gentleman to younger gentleman talk with our son and explained the repercussions for *our* family if we were to wed. *Our* son understands and only wishes for you to be his mama. As for Julia, she encouraged me to pursue you until you said yes. Even though she was not aware of your circumstances, I believe she would whole-heartedly approve. Because of your love for Henry and his for you."

Belle had tears in her eyes at his words. "Second, you must accept my lifestyle and the choices I make in my life. I will not stop the passions I believe in for the sake of status in the ton."

"Accepted. I should never have asked you to stop. I now understand why you have chosen the life you have and I shall support your decisions." Phillip spread the silk from her body, opening her to his pleasure. He ran a finger between her breasts, over her stomach.

Belle lost her train of thought at Phillip's touch. Her next question held no importance, but it would be instrumental on how she proceeded with her business. "And where shall we live?"

Phillip slid the robe off Belle's shoulders, letting it pool at her feet. His gaze trailed the length of her body. He would never tire of her. Phillip noticed the effect of his touch on Belle. Her nipples hardened, her body glowed, and her eyes clouded with desire. She was exquisite. Phillip teased his fingers around her nipples.

"A decision we can make together. I have enjoyed working in Parliament and would like to continue to do so. However, I would like to raise our children in the country. Perhaps we can share our time between both? Does that meet your approval?"

Belle moaned.

"Yes?"

"Mmm, yes." Yes, please touch me there, Phillip.

"Are you answering yes to where we shall live? Or are you answering yes to this?" Phillip asked, sliding his finger inside her wetness. He stroked her slowly, drawing out her pleasure.

"Yes, to whatever you desire."

"I desire only you, my sweet Belle."

Phillip rose and turned Belle around, facing the mirrors. Their reflection glowed in the firelight. He pulled Belle's hair back, kissing her neck. She arched back, pressing her body into his. Phillip met her gaze in the mirror. Phillip lifted her breasts in his hands, palming the globes and stroking her nipples. Belle closed her eyes.

"Open your eyes, Belle. I want you to watch our love."

Belle shook her head, keeping her eyes closed. Phillip dropped his hands and stepped away from her body. Her shyness kept her from releasing her inhibitions. She thought she could give him this, but her insecurities gave her doubt. Phillip never moved. His desire surrounded her. His need overpowered her senses. Even though Phillip never kissed or touched her, she sensed him. Soon, he traced a path down the curve of her back. His touch was light. Phillip coaxed Belle to open her eyes, his gaze unwavering.

Phillip slid inside her. Slowly. He whispered words, causing her to blush. His touch set her body aflame. Each kiss drew a desire for more. Belle watched their bodies become one. On each stroke, Phillip brought them to new heights.

Belle came alive in the mirror, dropping her façade and embracing her inner temptress. She dropped her head back against his shoulder and moved her body with his. Her hands stroked him from behind. With each thrust, he slid in deeper. Phillip filled his hands with her breasts.

"You fill my hands to perfection. Your nipples are meant for my fingers to play." Phillip whispered. He pinched her buds tightly. A warm blush graced her body.

"Watch our bodies dance, my love. We were made for each other." Phillip thrust into Belle. He swirled his hips around, increasing her pleasure. Belle pushed her buttocks into him, matching his dance. He groaned.

Phillip continued his onslaught of seduction. His strokes became harder. Deeper. His whispers more scandalous. The mirrors displayed their passion. She couldn't take her gaze away, even if she tried. They were memorizing to watch. Their bodies danced a waltz to the tune of their passion. Each dip and turn swayed together. Belle could hear the music in their moans. On the last note, Phillip dipped Belle over, clutching her hips, claiming her.

Phillip caught Belle in his arms, turning her to him. He kissed her with all his love. He would never get enough of her. Phillip vowed to spend the rest of their lives together making Belle happy. He didn't deserve her, but he would cherish her as she was meant to be.

Belle sighed into Phillip's kiss. She wrapped her arms around him and settled against the pillows. They talked long into the night about their plans. The heaviness of her life lifted from her heart. All she felt was happiness.

Chapter Nineteen

"Belle, my love, you must rise. I promised our son I would bring his Mama home for breakfast." Phillip sat on the edge of the bed, brushing Belle's hair from her eyes.

Belle rolled over, smiling at the mention of Henry. To have Phillip refer to him as their son warmed her heart.

"Yes, we must hurry. Please scoot, Phillip, I must rise." Belle swatted at Phillip to get out of her way.

"Humph, I am already being passed over for Henry. One would think you only agreed to my marriage proposal so you could be Henry's mama." Phillip rose from the bed, sulking away.

Belle wrapped the sheet around her body. "Well, I must admit, the boy holds my heart in his. If it were not for him, I would not have …" Belle teased.

"Would not have what?" Phillip turned.

"Found you again, my love." Belle stood on her tiptoes to place a kiss upon Phillip's lips.

"I would have searched the world over to find you. However, I will agree with you, the boy took all the work out of it for me." Phillip returned Belle's kiss.

Belle rushed to get dressed. She couldn't wait to start their life together. She had yet to explain to Phillip her plans for the brothel. All in due time. Belle was excited to share her vision with Phillip. She would make time later, now she only wanted to see Henry.

Phillip led Belle outside toward his carriage he had sent for. Before they reached it, Ned stepped out of the shadows.

"Delamont."

Phillip nodded a greeting. He should have known Ned would be nearby, protecting Belle. Phillip never brought forward his concern over Belle's neglection of her own welfare. A concern he would address later today.

Belle said, "Ned, we are on our way to Lord Delamont's to enjoy breakfast with our son. I shall return later today to discuss the plans for remolding. For now, if you could see to the removal of the wall coverings and curtains in the bedrooms. We must change the décor slightly."

"I will set the laborers on the task upon their arrival. In the meantime, enjoy your time with young Henry."

Phillip listened to the pride in Belle's voice when mentioning their son. Belle must have confided in Ned about Henry, for the man seemed to know how much Henry meant to Belle. While they discussed the renovation for her establishment, Phillip only listened with half an ear. A movement in the window distracted him. Perhaps a workman had arrived early. When smoke drifted from an open window Phillip knew something to be amiss.

"Fire! Ned, gather help," Phillip shouted.

Belle jumped at Phillip's command. Her gaze flew to the house and she saw the fire licking at the curtains. Her home was on fire—but in the shock came a sense of relief that nobody was inside. Ned flew down the street, calling out for help on his way to the fire pump. Only one thought flew in her head. She needed to retrieve a memento. It was all she had of her child. Belle ran into the house.

Phillip tore off his coat, assisting Ned in putting the fire out. Belle's neighbors poured out of their homes, eager to assist. Soon they formed a line and passed buckets of water to throw on the house. Once a system was in place, Phillip searched for Belle. She was nowhere to be found.

"Ned, where is Belle?"

"Is she in your carriage?"

Phillip rushed to the carriage, throwing open the doors. It sat empty. Phillip turned in horror to the house. She wouldn't have run back in, would she? Was she forced inside? Phillip tore off, running through the smoke, shouting for Belle. He ripped off his cravat, covering his mouth and nose. He heard Belle's scream. The farther he moved into the house, the less smoky it became. So far, they'd contained the fire to the front of the home. He needed to get out Belle before the fire trapped them.

He ran into her bedroom to discover his worst nightmare.

"So kind of you to join us, Lord Delamont," Lord Velden smirked.

Belle stood frightened, a knife held to her throat by Velden. When they had left, Belle had taken great care to her appearance. Now she stood with her hair pulled loose in Velden's grip. The dress ripped apart from her struggles. Blood dripped from her lips where Velden had dared to place his fist. Phillip controlled his anger so as not to harm Belle at Velden's hand.

"What can we do for you, Lord Velden?"

"I thought you were different, Lord Delamont."

"How so?"

"I thought with your political agenda you would not associate yourself with someone of Madame Bellerose's character. However, you proved me wrong by crawling in between her legs every night. Then again, I should admire you too. You achieved what no man in London has ever been able to. I am very conflicted where you are concerned."

"Release Belle now."

"Not until I seek my revenge." Velden said, lowering his knife. He backed away from Belle, yanking on her hair. Belle never even uttered a whimper. Velden cut the buttons off the back of Belle's dress. Once her dress draped open, his knife slit through the ties of her corset. He flipped the blade in between his fingers and ran the butt of the knife along her back. "Now that Belle is offering her services to the gentlemen of London, I am more than willing to sample her delights."

"If you touch her, I will end your life."

Velden brandished his knife, slicing it through the air.

"I hold the power, Delamont, not you."

Phillip advanced on Velden, coming within inches of them. Velden flashed his knife back to Belle's throat. Belle shook her head for Phillip to stop. He halted and took a step back.

"That is better. Now, after I find my pleasure with your whore, I will see to your demise. Such a tragedy it will be. A lover's spat, gone awry. Your jealously over her profession caused you to slash her throat and burn her establishment to the ground. I must let you go though, I cannot have a lord of the realm's death on my hands. My revenge toward your interference with my dealings to destroy Madame Bellerose will be in the charges brought against you toward her death. By the time they dismiss the charges, your reputation will be in tatters. No lord will respect your word or allow you near their daughters. Your son will bear the shame for years to come."

"Please allow Lord Delamont to leave. You may seek your revenge on me, but let him return to his son an innocent party," Belle pleaded.

"You have no room for negotiation. I visited your establishment for years, supporting your business. You allowed sponsorship for many of my colleagues. I contributed to your success. And how do you repay my kindness? You stage a card game to exile me from England. Is that any way to repay a friend?" Velden asked, yanking the dress and corset from Belle's body.

"I have never considered you a friend, Lord Velden. 'Tis true your generosity over the years helped to contribute to my success. You always walked the line where I could never turn you away. I did not approve of your dealings, but you broke no rules for me to deny you access. Until you threatened Lady Kathleen. You made many enemies in London, and when they came to me for help on taking you down, far be it for me to refuse."

"You bitch." Velden swung out an arm, knocking Belle against the vanity.

Phillip watched Belle's head slam into the wooden frame. His need to comfort her would have to wait. He advanced on Velden, slamming him against the wall. The lord slashed out with his knife, catching Phillip across the arm. When Velden took another swipe at Phillip, he knocked the knife from Velden's hand. Phillip then unleashed the anger he held back since coming upon Velden holding Belle captive. His fists pounded on Velden, one after another, even after Velden fell to the floor.

A pair of arms pulled Phillip from Velden. Phillip turned around swinging, ready to defend Belle and himself. Wildeburg and Beckwith pulled him away, while Holdenburg dragged Velden to his feet. Phillip shook himself free, turning to Belle's aid. Sheffield stood with Belle in his arms, his suit coat covering her. He walked over and laid her in Phillip's arms.

"Get her out of here before this house falls in," ordered Sheffield.

They rushed from the house to the safety of Belle's garden. Beckwith and Holdenburg stood guard over Velden, waiting for the local magistrate. Phillip had knocked the man unconscious. Ned came around the house and gave a report on how they had the fire under control. Wildeburg followed Ned to the damage to give him new directions. Still, Belle had not come to. Phillip gripped her hand, noticing for the first time that Belle clutched a silver locket. He tried to pry it loose, but her grasp only tightened.

"It holds a locket of your son's hair," Sheffield explained.

"That explains her reason to return inside."

"It is the only memento she has of him. Belle always wears the chain around her neck."

"I have never seen it before."

"No, I do not suppose she would wear it around you. It would have caused you to ask too many questions that she was not yet ready to answer."

"I owe you an apology."

"Well, let's hear it."

"Serious?"

"Yes, I want to listen to your explanation for this apology. Phee told me to accept it graciously, however, I prefer to hear you grovel."

"You are a vindictive man, Sheffield."

"So I have been told."

Phillip sighed. He might as well grovel at the man's feet or he would never find peace. "I apologize for my ungentlemanly disregard for your friendship with Belle, and my accusations toward your character. I am also indebted to the protection and care you gave Belle."

"Ah, I love having someone in my debt."

"For the love of God, just accept the poor man's apology, Sheffield," Belle groaned.

"Very well. You are forgiven, old chap." Sheffield laughed.

"How are you, my love?" asked Phillip, cupping her cheek in his hand.

Belle pressed her lips against his hand. "I ache something fierce. But I will survive. Lord Velden?"

"He is being taken into custody. The man will no longer be a threat to our lives," Sheffield answered.

"That is a relief. Now, explain how you came to our rescue," said Belle.

"Your friends arrived at Delamont's residence at Henry's invitation to join your family for breakfast this morning, one that he issued yesterday."

"My son made no such offer."

Sheffield laughed. "Yes, he did. Your distraction led you not to notice. Anyway, as I was saying, upon our arrival, Henry informed us you had not returned home. We waited and when you made no appearance, we grew worried. The ladies stayed with Henry, while we came to investigate. Once we arrived and saw the fire, we knew you were in danger. Upon rushing in, we saw you beating Velden to within an inch of his life and Belle knocked out on the floor. The rest is history. Now, if you will excuse me, I will assist Wildeburg with your home."

Phillip leaned his forehead against Belle's. "You frightened me near death. Please promise you will never be so reckless with your life again."

"I promise," Belle whispered, her voice scratchy from the smoke.

"Can I see?" Phillip took the locket from Belle's hand.

Belle watched Phillip open the locket with care. He touched the hair and gently closed the locket again. Phillip brought the necklace to his lips and placed a kiss upon it. Then he lifted Belle's hair and slid the necklace around her neck, holding it against Belle's heart.

"Will you wear it again for me?"

Belle nodded, too choked to speak. Belle had listened to Sheffield explain to Phillip about the locket while she came to. He expressed not an ounce of jealousy at Sheffield's knowledge of the necklace. Only acceptance. Belle covered his hand.

"I love you, my sweet Belle."

"I love you, Phillip."

"Your business will need to stay closed longer than you anticipated, I'm afraid. We can hire an architect to help reconstruct the layout."

"I already hired an architect to make some necessary changes. We can contact him on the morrow. I am closing Madame Bellerose's establishment and reopening my doors to help train women with no means. I want to teach them skills so they can find employment in more reputable positions. It has been a dream of mine for years."

"That is why the sign said you were closed for remodeling."

"Yes, I meant to tell you last night, but …" Belle blushed a beautiful shade of pink.

"Mmm, you became distracted." Phillip brushed open the coat covering Belle. He slid the strap off her chemise. "You are an amazing woman, my love. I am in awe of you." Phillip bent over and kissed Belle's bare shoulder.

"Since we missed breakfast, are you at least going to feed us lunch?" Sheffield asked, having returned unnoticed. The fire was out.

Belle gasped, pulling the coat closed and turning into Phillip. Phillip answered Sheffield, laughing at Belle's shyness. He rose from the bench following Sheffield to the waiting carriages. There would be time later to shower Belle with his devotion. For now he would see to her comfort and find a way to rid himself of her friends. Nay, they were now his friends too.

Epilogue

Within a week, Belle and Phillip were happily married. Henry stood between them at the altar, marking his acceptance of their marriage. Their friends gathered around them in Belle's garden. The wedding guests were a strange mixture, but one that held no qualms on the status of their rank in the hierarchy of life. From her employees, to her neighborhood friends, to her dear friends of the peerage. They all came together to offer their love. Even Sidney and Sophia's parents offered their support of the union. Along with Rory and Kathleen's mother, and Dallis's grandmother, Lady Ratcliff. When the Duke and Duchess of Norbrooke arrived with a donation toward Belle's new venture, Belle broke down in tears. They vowed their support of her entry into society. They owed her a debt of gratitude at being instrumental in bringing their son, Lord Holdenburg, and Kathleen together.

Throughout the day, Phillip never left Belle's side. Nor did she want him to. Belle stood back from the crowd, smiling at the overwhelming sight. More tears came to her eyes often. Phillip stood behind Belle, wrapping his arms around her waist.

"No tears on your wedding day."

"Even if they are tears of happiness?"

"I shall allow those."

Belle turned in his arms. "You have made all my dreams come true today, Lord Delamont."

"Your dreams have only just begun, Lady Delamont."

"Lady Delamont, I like the sound of that."

"Music to my ears, my dear. But do you know what I would love to hear?" Phillip asked.

"No." Belle looked suspiciously at him.

"I would love to hear you shout Lord Delamont to the rafters while I ravish your lovely body," Phillip whispered in her ear.

His scandalous words still made her blush, but she'd learned to enjoy teasing him in return.

"Only if you shout Lady Delamont when I ..." Belle finished, whispering in Phillip's ear.

Phillip growled, lifting Belle over his shoulder, and striding out of the garden.

"Sheffield take care of Henry," Phillip shouted over his shoulder.

"Phillip, put me down this instant." Belle hung upside-down, mortified at Phillip's behavior. She couldn't look toward her guests without dying of embarrassment. Their laughter and shouts of congratulations mingled in the air.

"Now, now, my lovely Belle, you promised that you would only call me Lord Delamont this evening," Phillip said, dumping Belle on the carriage seat. With swift instructions to the driver, he kneeled before Belle, sliding up her skirts.

Her scoundrel of a husband's desire would be forever her demise. Belle became entranced with the man who'd held her heart in his hands. She had held onto his love all these years and would continue to do so.

It did not take long for Belle to succumb to Phillip's charms.

"Oh, Lord Delamont."

Belle finally received her happily ever after.

~~~

Dear Lovely Readers,

I hope you have enjoyed reading the Tricking the Scoundrels books as much I have loved writing them. When I first sat down to write Whom Shall I Kiss.., it was meant to be a stand-alone novel. But once I started adding characters, I wanted to give them their own happily ever after. I never meant to give Belle her own story, until after I finished writing, I Shall Love the Earl. Then I realized how instrumental she was in helping everyone find love. She had her own heartache that needed to be told. Her story brought a fitting ending to the series, that I hoped you enjoyed reading. Thank you for reading the books and all your kind words.

Happy Reading,

Laura

~~~

Visit my website www.lauraabarnes.com to join my mailing list.

~~~

"Thank you for reading The Forgiven Scoundrel. Gaining exposure as an independent author relies mostly on word-of-mouth, so if you have the time and inclination, please consider leaving a short review wherever you can."

~~~

P.S. Don't forget to check out the first book in my new series: How the Lady Charmed the Marquess (Matchmaking Madness #1)

Desire other books to read by Laura A. Barnes

Enjoy these other historical romances:

<u>Fate of the Worthingtons Series</u>
The Tempting Minx
The Seductive Temptress
The Fiery Vixen
The Siren's Gentleman

~~~~~

<u>Matchmaking Madness Series:</u>
How the Lady Charmed the Marquess
How the Earl Fell for His Countess
How the Rake Tempted the Lady
How the Scot Stole the Bride
How the Lady Seduced the Viscount
How the Lord Married His Lady

~~~~~

<u>Tricking the Scoundrels Series:</u>
Whom Shall I Kiss… An Earl, A Marquess, or A Duke?
Whom Shall I Marry… An Earl or A Duke?
I Shall Love the Earl
The Scoundrel's Wager
The Forgiven Scoundrel

~~~~~

Romancing the Spies Series:

Rescued By the Captain

Rescued By the Spy

Rescued By the Scot

Author Laura A. Barnes

International selling author Laura A. Barnes fell in love with writing in the second grade. After her first creative writing assignment, she knew what she wanted to become. Many years went by with Laura filling her head full of story ideas and some funny fish songs she wrote while fishing with her family. Thirty-seven years later, she made her dreams a reality. With her debut novel *Rescued By the Captain*, she has set out on the path she always dreamed about.

When not writing, Laura can be found devouring her favorite romance books. Laura is married to her own Prince Charming (who for some reason or another thinks the heroes in her books are about him) and they have three wonderful children and two sweet grandbabies. Besides her love of reading and writing, Laura loves to travel. With her passport stamped in England, Scotland, and Ireland; she hopes to add more countries to her list soon.

While Laura isn't very good on the social media front, she loves to hear from her readers. You can find her on the following platforms:

You can visit her at ***www.lauraabarnes.com*** to join her mailing list.

Website: **http://www.lauraabarnes.com**

Amazon: **https://amazon.com/author/lauraabarnes**

Goodreads: **https://www.goodreads.com/author/show/16332844.Laura_A_Barnes**

Facebook: **https://www.facebook.com/AuthorLauraA.Barnes/**

Instagram: **https://www.instagram.com/labarnesauthor/**

Twitter: **https://twitter.com/labarnesauthor**

TikTok: **https://www.tiktok.com/@labarnesauthor**

BookBub: **https://www.bookbub.com/profile/laura-a-barnes**

Printed in Great Britain
by Amazon